HIS MATE BY DEFIANCE

LUNETTI PACK 4

MEL AITCHESS

Copyright © 2026 by Mel Aitchess

All rights reserved.

No part of this book may be reproduced in any form or by any electronic or mechanical means, including information storage and retrieval systems, without written permission from the author, except for the use of brief quotations in a book review.

ISBN: 978-1-0670227-8-5 (ebook)

ISBN: 978-1-0670227-9-2 (paperback)

Cover by Camberion

Proofread by JennReadsMMBooks

❀ Formatted with Vellum

AUTHOR NOTE

This novel is an MM, mafia shifter, paranormal romance.

It contains extensive swearing, graphic sex, and graphic violence. For a more fulsome list of content warnings, head over to my website. There is knotting (and other paranormal fun) but no mpreg in this world.

The series is set in a fictional city in a world like ours with familiar countries and oblivious humans.

I released a short story for my newsletter, TO DEFY HIS MATE, that told the story of Rafe and Adri's first meeting. I've included that short story and the last chapter of the previous book as prologues so you don't miss anything if you haven't read them, but otherwise you can just skip to chapter one.

Enjoy!

Love, Mel xx

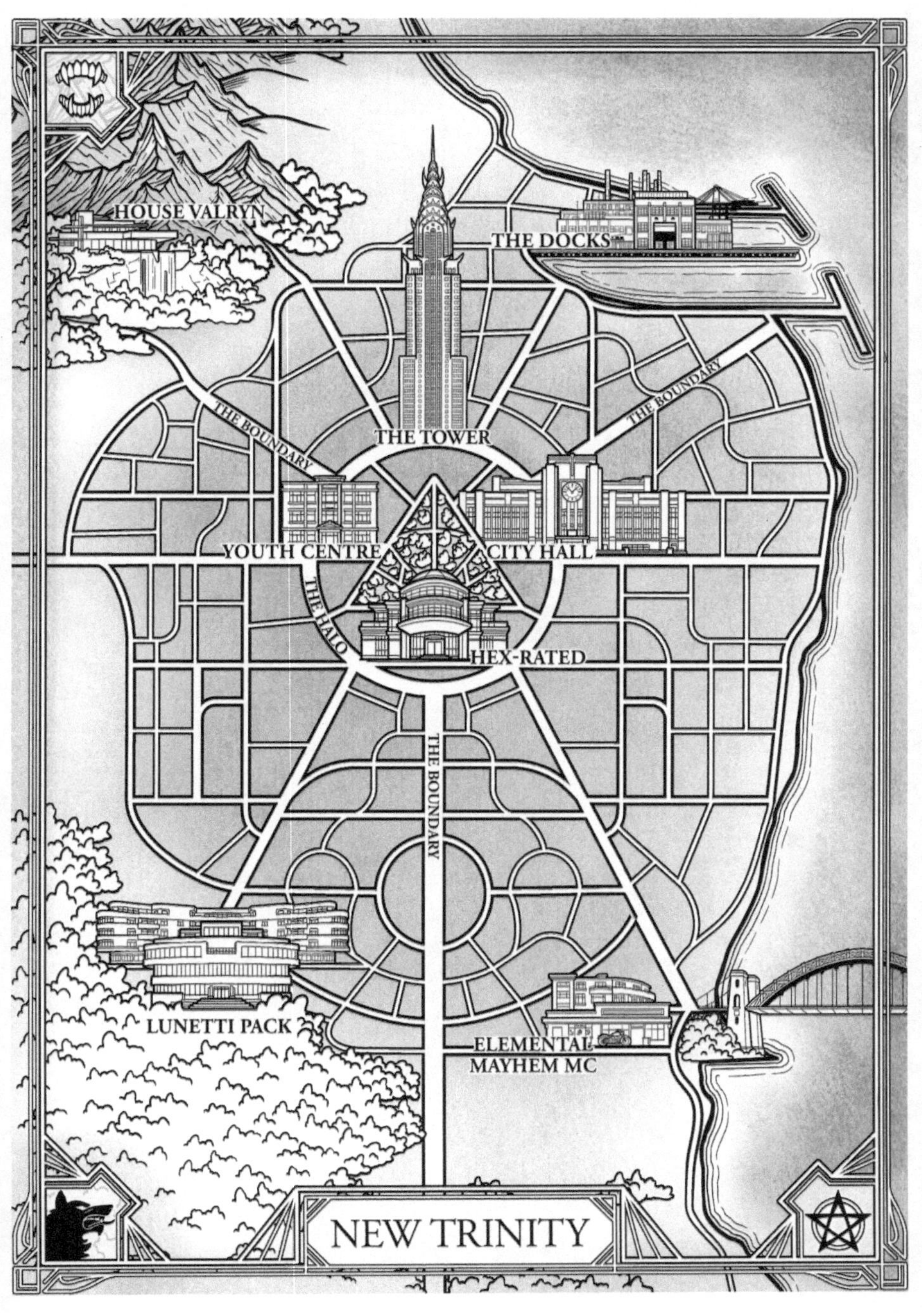
HOUSE VALRYN
THE DOCKS
THE TOWER
THE BOUNDARY
THE BOUNDARY
YOUTH CENTRE
CITY HALL
THE HALO
HEX-RATED
THE BOUNDARY
LUNETTI PACK
ELEMENTAL
MAYHEM MC
NEW TRINITY

TO DEFY HIS MATE: RAFE

"Damn, sweetheart. If you can't lose without breaking both your legs, you have no business in the cage," Rafe growled, taking in the broken and bloodied form lying on the concrete floor of a back room of tonight's illegal venue.

Every instinct in him was screaming to scoop up the young jaguar shifter into his arms. The fighter was compact and sleekly muscular. Exquisitely beautiful despite the bruises and grazes on his otherwise smooth dark skin. His head and face were both shaved but with just enough stubble to abrade Rafe in the best way once he was healed enough to invite to play.

"It's not as if I have a ch—" The jaguar's words cut off as the emerald green of his gaze flicked behind Rafe to where the manager had just appeared in the doorway.

Was the jaguar here against his will? The Lunetti Pack might be the shifter equivalent of the mafia, but they had no patience for slavery of any kind. Nothing was more sacred than freedom to a shifter. He'd have to have a quiet word with his Alpha, Marco, when he was done here before the transitory fighting ring left the shifter sector of New Trinity for Cruor Coven territory. The vampire coven trafficked in flesh and blood and wouldn't give a fuck if a shifter was being held against his will.

"Who said he lost? Just patch him up, Doc," the manager, Garth, snapped.

Garth was a dick. The only reason Rafe had even answered his call was because he'd never let someone die in his arms again if he could help it. It was just as well, too, because the second he'd caught the scent of this jaguar, he'd known the young shifter was *his*. Rafe's wolf was practically howling inside his chest to claim him, but the guy looked barely legal, so his wolf was just going to have to fucking wait.

"There's nothing here that won't heal on its own with a decent meal and a good night's sleep," Rafe said, pretending an ambivalence he wasn't feeling to try and puzzle out why he'd been called.

Shifter healing was excellent. His services as a doctor had been much less in demand since the last shifter war ended decades earlier and the agreement between the three crime families of New Trinity was established. Most of his time was spent in his free clinic dealing with witches who couldn't afford treatment from their own kind and the supernatural street kids and homeless whose biggest health issue was lack of food.

"I need Crusher back out in the ring within the hour. Make it happen," Garth said. A moment later, his presence was gone. The vampire was swift and silent enough that Rafe had to rely on scent and instinct to sense he'd left.

Rafe drew in a deep breath to keep his fury from shining through as his eyes stayed locked on the beautiful wrecked body lying before him. Everything in him rebelled at the thought of healing the young man only to send him out to be broken again, but there was no way Rafe would leave him suffering a moment longer.

"Sorry you have to waste your power on me," the jaguar mumbled, turning his head away.

"It's never a waste to ease someone's pain," Rafe said, reaching out to take the jaguar's hand in his and ignoring the look of surprise he received for his words.

He had to push another wave of anger down as his thumb brushed over cracked and bruised knuckles. Reaching deep inside for the well of healing power inside him, he pushed it down through their connection and into the young man lying on the floor, letting it flow like moonlight into every broken bone and swollen tissue.

The jaguar's quickly stifled cry as his fractured shins started knitting back together was a knife to his gut, and he cast around for something, anything, he could say to distract the man from the pain.

"So, *Crusher*? Really?" Rafe asked, surprised and delighted when a delicate flush spread up the jaguar's neck to his cheeks. The young man was a good four inches shorter than him, not a hulking brute like his fighting name would suggest.

"Yes, really. When I shift, there's no one with a stronger bite," he said, but he didn't sound all that proud about it.

"What's your real name, sweetheart?" Rafe asked, only half paying attention as he continued the delicate and exhausting work of making sure his healing magic made it to every bit of damage. He couldn't send the jaguar back into the ring with a weakness.

"Don't call me that. I'm not some soft little thing looking for a fucking Daddy," he snarled.

Surprise had Rafe freezing his progress before he forced his focus back on what he was doing. "Who said anything about a Daddy?"

"You're sitting right next to me. I can smell your arousal. I can see the pity and the saviour complex in your eyes, old man. You wouldn't be the first one to try."

Rafe's jaw clenched tight with rage at the thought of someone trying to take what was his, and it was only decades of professionalism that stopped him from hauling his patient onto his lap. The reminder of their age difference didn't help. He knew he didn't look old despite the grey streaks in his hair that matched the silver in his wolf's fur. Shifters were immortal unless killed, and they didn't age past their thirties.

The petulant words were a stark reminder that his jaguar was too young to commit to what Rafe wanted from him, as was the jaguar's apparent lack of awareness of the potential mating bond between them. Cat shifters were naturally independent and never felt the draw to mate as strongly, so the obliviousness was probably genuine. Either way, it wasn't the right time for them, no matter how much Rafe ached with need. His wolf growled inside his head in protest.

"If you don't want me to call you sweetheart, give me something else to call you. And how old are you? Are you even old enough to fight?"

The jaguar scoffed. "It's not like the fights are legal, anyway. There aren't any rules. I'm twenty, and I've been fighting for years. If I'm old enough to drink and fuck, I'm old enough to fight."

Fucking hell. Rafe had more than four decades on this guy. Intellectually, he knew it wasn't much in the scheme of things. In shifter terms, Rafe was still in his youth, but despite the immature attitude the jaguar was displaying, there was something in the deep green of his eyes that spoke to a worldliness based on harsh life experience. He'd clearly never had a chance to be young and innocent. Rafe's need to claim was tempered by an even deeper need to take him home and let him discover life outside of this violence. To let him run with the young wolves on their pack lands and study at the local university.

"If you're here against your will, I can help you out. Well, the pack can help you out. I'm more a lover than a fighter," Rafe said.

"I don't need you to save me."

Rafe shrugged and pretended a nonchalance he didn't feel. He wasn't going to get anywhere by bullying the jaguar like everyone else in his life likely did. He needed to play the long game.

"Okay."

As the last bruise faded from the jaguar's face, Rafe reluctantly dropped his hand and leaned back to stretch tense neck muscles. If he hadn't had supernatural hearing, he would've missed the name when it came.

"Adrien," the man whispered.

It was a gift. One far better than any thank you he'd ever received. Rafe smiled. Adrien. It suited the jaguar so much more than *Crusher*.

"My friends call me Rafe," he said.

"Good to know, Doc," Adrien replied, sparking a bark of laughter from him.

Their eyes met, and Adrien's lips quirked up in the faintest of smiles. Rafe's pupils dilated and his breath caught in his lungs as he watched the move. What he wouldn't give to nip at the lush flesh there, to trace it with his tongue and taste the man whose scent was making him drunk with lust.

Shaking his head, he got himself under control and rose back to his feet, holding out a hand to help Adrien stand. The jaguar ignored it and sprung up with a fluid grace that screamed his feline shifter nature to the world.

"How do you feel?" Rafe asked.

Adrien stepped back and twisted himself into various stretches before dropping into a fighting stance to snap out a rapid-fire combination of punches and kicks. Rafe was mesmerised. His jaguar was shirtless and only wearing a pair of thin, satiny boxing shorts. He might be less bulky than most wolf shifters, but the power in his body was evident in every carefully controlled and targeted move. His biceps bulged and his abs flexed as he used his entire body to propel his strikes.

"I'm good. Thanks, Doc," Adrien said when he was finished.

"You're fucking perfect, is what you are," Rafe growled before his brain could catch up.

Adrien smirked at him and stalked closer. Rafe let himself be backed up until he was pressed against the nearest wall, caged in by Adrien's arms. "I don't need a Daddy to save me, but I could call you Daddy for the night," he purred.

Rafe swallowed hard, but before he could reply, a voice called from the hallway.

"Fight's in five, Crusher!"

"Mmm… hold that thought, Doc," Adrien said.

As Adrien moved to pull away, Rafe's hand shot out to grip his nape and keep him close. Leaning forward, he nuzzled into the young man's neck—scent-marking him—before drawing in a deep breath of his jungle scent. Adrien's chest vibrated against him with a deep purr as he tipped his head to the side to give Rafe better access, baring his throat in the process. Rafe groaned at the unintentional submission. It was all he could do not to bite him on the spot.

"Meet me in the showers when I'm done," Adrien growled.

Then the jaguar shifter was speeding out the door and gone. *Dammit.* Was he really going to stick around until Adrien was done fighting when he was about ready to drop from exhaustion from expending so much power healing? Banging his head on the wall behind him, he swore at his own stupidity. Of course he was. No way could he pass up what Adrien was offering. But even worse than that, his wolf wouldn't let him leave when Adrien might need him.

Fucking hell. He was so screwed. He didn't even bother going out to watch the fight, knowing he'd be unable to keep himself under control if Adrien was hurt again. Instead, he slunk off into the decrepit old changing rooms and lay back on a wide wooden bench with his arm over his face to block the harsh fluorescent lights.

He must've drifted off because he woke to the brush of cool air on his chest, followed by a wet-hot suction on his nipple that had him arching with a cry as he reached down to grip the back of Adrien's neck. Adrien had crawled up his body and was crouched over him. Rafe's moan echoed against the cold concrete walls as Adrien kept up his sensual assault before tugging off him with a pop that grazed sharp fangs against the sensitive skin, leaving Rafe gasping.

"What the fuck were you doing falling asleep here? Anyone could've attacked you," Adrien growled, before bending down to give his other nipple the same treatment as his hand traced up Rafe's ribs to start pinching and tweaking the one he'd only just released.

"Awww, are you punishing me, baby?" Rafe teased as his body thrummed with pleasure and pain.

Adrien was right. He definitely shouldn't have fallen asleep in the back room of an illegal fighting ring. It was unlikely any of the fighters or organisers would bite the hand that healed them, but it was always possible one of the punters would get back here and not recognise him. He'd been more drained than he realised.

"Someone needs to," Adrien said, trailing bruising kisses up his chest and neck.

Adrien's body was hot and sweaty against him from his fight, the delicious musk of his scent almost overwhelming. A quick scan with his magic reassured him the fighter had no serious injuries needing attention.

"Stop doctoring me already," Adrien complained, sensing his power.

Wrapping a leg around Adrien's hip, Rafe used his larger size as leverage to flip them over so the jaguar shifter was underneath him before leaning down to finally claim those lips. He was thwarted at the last second by Adrien turning his face away so he ended up kissing his jaw. Biting back a growl of frustration, he gripped Adrien's chin and forced him to look at him.

"I have rules if we do this," Adrien said before Rafe could give voice to his frustration.

Drawing in a deep breath, Rafe jerked a nod. His wolf was riding him hard to fuck, to bite, to claim. Rules were good. Rules were *necessary*. They'd stop things from getting out of hand.

"One night only. No repeats. No saviour complex. We get each other off. Then you fuck off," Adrien said.

Rafe's nostrils flared as he bit his tongue hard enough to draw blood. What the fuck? There was no way he would agree to that, and he had no intention of lying to the man he would one day claim as his mate. Once would never be enough. He wasn't going to leave Adrien fighting here where he'd be used until the day his shifter healing wasn't enough and he died in the ring.

"No." Rafe was sent flying across the room before he'd finished biting out the word, slamming into the wall of the nearest shower stall.

"Wait!" he cried as Adrien stalked toward the exit.

The jaguar became a blur of motion, and then Rafe was looking up at the long, exquisite length of his body where he towered above him.

"Those are the rules. Take it or leave it," Adrien snapped.

Rafe could hear the desperate need in his jaguar's voice. Could see his hard length straining his shorts. The scent of their combined arousal filled the air. Pushing away from where he'd sprawled against the wall, Rafe got his knees under him so he could nuzzle into the join where Adrien's thigh met his groin, drawing in a deep, intoxicating breath. His hands traced up the smooth skin of the shifter's legs, teasing their way ever higher.

"What if only one of us gets off?" he asked, holding Adrien's gaze as he reached up to tug his shorts and boxers down to remove the last barrier holding him back from what he wanted.

Adrien's head tipped back with a moan. He huffed a soft, wry laugh as Rafe began tracing lines along the deep vee of his muscles with his tongue, kissing and licking him everywhere except the proud hard length of his shaft that was bobbing like the perfect temptation right in front of his face.

"Are you seriously looking for loopholes right now?" Adrien gasped as Rafe moved his way down to start lapping at his balls that were already high and tight against his body.

"Would you seriously walk away from this?" Rafe asked, and then he turned his head and sucked Adrien's beautiful cock into his mouth.

The sweet taste of pre-cum burst across his tongue as he used his hand to roll back Adrien's foreskin so he could lave at the sensitive head. He groaned as he felt the ridges swelling along Adrien's cock. He'd never been fucked by a feline shifter before, but he'd heard they felt amazing. The vibration of the noises he was making had Adrien shuddering and he was rewarded for his efforts with a string of curses and a fist tightening in his hair.

Using his knee to budge Adrien's stance wider, he reached up to massage behind his balls as he pulled against the grip on his hair to try and take him deeper. A strangled whine of protest escaped him when the grip didn't loosen and he pulled back to glare up at Adrien.

"Fuck, you're desperate for it, aren't you? Why won't you just agree to the rules so we can actually fuck?" Adrien asked, the slightest tremor in his voice. Sliding a thumb along Rafe's lip, Adrien pushed the digit into his mouth so he could swirl his tongue around it and suck.

"Loophole, remember?" Rafe said, shifting where he knelt and reaching down to adjust himself so his straining erection didn't end up with a permanent mark where it was pushing against the zip of his slacks.

"Only if you don't come," Adrien said, tightening the grip he had on Rafe's hair.

Rafe smirked. He'd never been so hard in his life, but if this was what it took so that he didn't have to promise he'd walk away, he could keep himself under control. There were some advantages to being a little older, at least. He doubted he would've managed it at Adrien's age. Shifter libidos were high and their possessive instincts and senses made everything more intense. It took time to adjust once those needs awakened.

"Don't pretend like you're not going to get off on denying me," Rafe said.

Adrien's gaze darkened and his pupils dilated until only the thinnest circle of green was visible around them. Rafe understood. If anyone needed the feeling of control, it would be this young man trapped unwillingly in a violent world.

"You think you can take it?" Adrien asked, his breaths turning to pants and his heart starting to race.

"For you? I will take it all. All your pain. All your desire. Everything. It's all mine," Rafe growled.

"Aren't you like a big fuck-off wolf alpha or something?" Adrien asked, yearning in his eyes.

"Or something," Rafe said.

"Open your mouth."

Rafe kept his eyes on Adrien's as he did as he'd commanded, parting his lips and letting his tongue loll out. He'd never let a lover take control like this before. Never wanted to. But he'd do anything for this man he barely knew, and that thought was as terrifying as it was arousing.

Adrien seemed entranced, staring at his mouth like it was the answer to everything wrong in his world.

"Are you sure?" Adrien whispered, leaning closer despite himself.

"Give me your pain," Rafe urged, flicking at the tip of Adrien's cock with his tongue.

The move unleashed his jaguar. He barely had time to inhale a deep breath before that delicious, huge, ridged cock was sliding into his mouth and down his throat.

"Fuck, look at you," Adrien gasped, reverence in his voice as he used his grip on Rafe's hair to thrust into him.

Groaning, Rafe frantically undid his belt so he could grip the base of his cock hard and stave off his orgasm. *Dammit.* The skin where his knot would form once they mated was hypersensitive and tingling, making it really fucking hard to use his hand there as a makeshift cock ring.

Adrien's laugh turned a little evil. "You alright there, Doc?"

There was nothing for it. He needed to make his jaguar come, and he needed to do it now or he was going to lose it. Sliding a finger into his mouth alongside Adrien's cock, he toyed with the shifter's ridges as he got it nice and slick. Adrien might be controlling how deep and fast Rafe sucked him off, but he hadn't restrained his arms. This time. The thought made him moan and a shiver went through his body that had the jaguar fucking his face harder.

Reaching between Adrien's legs, he circled his now slick fingers around his hole, brushing and tapping over it again and again. Adrien's rhythm faltered and he would've smiled if he'd been able to around the huge cock as Adrien pulled back until just the tip was in his mouth to chase the pleasure he was teasing with his hand.

"Fuck yes," Adrien gasped, as Rafe finally relented and pushed a finger into the tight heat of his body.

A tortured moan left him as Adrien became a thing of pure need and pleasure, thrusting down into his throat and then back onto his finger. Rafe couldn't last much longer. His cock was so hard it was an exquisite ache. Even his strangling grip around its base wasn't enough to stop it from throbbing with the first signs of an impending release.

Resisting the next pull on his hair, he kept Adrien's cock lodged deep in his throat, swallowing and moaning around it as he let his mouth vibrate with his muffled screams of pleasure. Releasing his own shaft so he had both hands free to pleasure his jaguar, he started tugging and playing with Adrien's balls while he slid another finger into his ass alongside the first. Crooking his fingers, he massaged and pressed against that spot inside Adrien that was making him thrum with need relentlessly.

"Fuck, Rafe. Please. Don't stop."

Adrien's words devolved into an unintelligible string of swearwords and endearments as his whole body strained forward before he finally tensed in release, letting loose with a roar Rafe was sure everyone else in the building heard as the shaft in his mouth pulsed with wave after wave of cum.

Whining, he chased after the delicious taste as Adrien pulled out of his mouth before he'd finished, but his complaint turned to another groan of satisfaction as Adrien reached down to furiously finish jerking himself. The jaguar shifter sent stripes of cum streaming down Rafe's neck and chest, dripping down the gap where the top buttons of his shirt were undone—marking him. Adrien might not be consciously aware of the potential mating bond between them, but this behaviour—drenching Rafe in his scent—showed just how much his jaguar was feeling the draw between them.

Holy fuck. Was Rafe really still fully dressed while his jaguar was standing there buck naked? It took everything in him not to come hands-free from the image as he processed the sensory overload. Closing his eyes, he gasped deep, panting breaths in through his mouth as he slumped back against the cool tile. He heard rather than saw Adrien slide down the wall to rest beside him.

"Want a hand with that?" Adrien asked.

Rafe opened his eyes and almost lost control again when he took in the sight of the thoroughly fucked-out man oozing satisfaction as he eyed up Rafe's throbbing erection like he was starving.

"Only if you're giving up your rules."

"Not on your life."

Adrien reached toward his aching cock and it took everything Rafe had to bat the jaguar shifter's hand away.

"Then I'm good," he said.

Adrien's look was incredulous. "You can't be serious."

"Thank you for trusting me with your pleasure," Rafe said, leaning forward to press a kiss to Adrien's cheek.

Then he did the hardest thing he'd ever done. He walked away.

TO DEFY HIS MATE: ADRI

It had been a week since the shower that shall not be mentioned and Adri still couldn't get the damn wolf shifter out of his head. He'd been certain Rafe would succumb to his charms and he'd be able to hold him to his rules.

Not Rafe, he reminded himself, the doc. They weren't friends. He'd been certain *the doc* would succumb. Just like he'd been certain the doc would do as he'd asked and fuck off once they were done.

Except, the damn doc had walked away unsatisfied after giving him the best orgasm of his life. Which meant Rafe wasn't walking away at all. And now Adri hadn't seen him for a week and he didn't know what was going on.

Shaking his head in disgust at himself, he went back to pounding the kickboxing bag in front of him, pouring all his pain into it, just like he'd poured all his pain into Rafe's mouth.

Fucking hell. Why did every thought lead back to *him*?

"Adri?" a quiet voice called from the doorway.

Adri looked over and forced a smile on his face he wasn't

feeling. He didn't want to scare Jay. Despite being over six feet with muscles on his muscles, the young vampire was too kind for this life. He'd been turned against his will to be used in the fighting ring and Adri had been protecting him ever since. Making sure the kid, because that's what he was even though Jay was older than him, survived.

Adri knew what it was like to be thrust into the supernatural world unprepared. He'd been raised by humans and had no idea he was a shifter until he was kidnapped as a teen. It had been stupidly unlucky. The vampires had thought he was human and intended to traffic him. They'd panicked when they realised what he was and sold him to Garth because Garth was a fucking asshole and thought a clueless jaguar shifter would make for some light comic relief before the real fights started. He'd shown Garth how wrong he was when the guy he was fighting walked away with eight broken ribs puncturing his lungs like a pin cushion. Which was how Adri got his nickname—Crusher.

"Yeah, kid? What's up?" Adri asked.

"There's a dead body in the common room and some lady told us to go meet there. I'm scared," Jay whispered.

Fuck. What the hell was going on? He needed to get there fast. Jay wasn't the only one among the fighters he looked after and he knew they'd be as stressed as the vampire was. Adri was across the room in less than a second, tucking the big vampire into his arm even though Adri's head only came up to Jay's shoulder.

"Come on. I'll take care of it," he said, not at all sure he'd be able to.

The first thing he noticed as he stepped into the common room was the overwhelming smell of viscera. A quick glance in the direction it was coming from confirmed what he'd suspected. After years of being an asshole to everyone he met, someone had finally taken Garth out. The vampire's head was resting on a side table. His intestines had been draped around it like some kind of floral arrangement and the rest of his body had been left slumped underneath.

Well. That was certainly a message. If only he knew what kind.

Tipping his chin in greeting to a couple of the older fighters in the centre of the room, he made his way to the far corner where a cluster of younger shifters stood nervously. They were all wolves, the most common shifters in the city. Jaguars didn't have packs like wolves, but he knew these young ones needed the reassurance their instincts craved, so he pretended for them. Reaching out, he squeezed their shoulders and scented them before nudging Jay to join them so he could place himself between the young fighters and the rest of the room as they waited in silence to find out who their next owner would be.

They didn't have to wait long.

Three wolf shifters swept into the room from the direction of Garth's office and a wave of dominance crashed over them from the one in the lead. Every wolf in the room immediately bared their throat. Adri just glared. He wasn't a damn wolf and he didn't owe anyone his submission. He'd never seen the guy in person before, but everyone in New Trinity knew who he was. Six foot five. More intimidating than any fighter in the room. A suit that cost more than Adri made for the fighting ring in a month and that irritating Mediterranean tall, dark and sternly handsome beauty.

This was Marco—Alpha of the Lunetti Pack.

Fucking Rafe. He should've known the doc wouldn't be able to help himself. Rafe must've gone running to his Alpha to fix things and now the fucking shifter mafia had taken over the fighting ring. How was that any better than Garth? A criminal was a criminal.

On either side of Marco stood two of his pack—a russet-haired man whose gaze tracked every movement and threat in the room, and a female shifter who oozed her own alpha dominance, although nowhere near the level of Marco's.

"As you've no doubt guessed, the ring is now owned by the Lunetti Pack. Viviana will be managing things from here on. Any debt you owed to that piece of shit vampire is now owed to me. Fuck with me and I'll bury you," Marco growled.

The woman at Marco's side stepped forward as he finished speaking, bowing her head to him before turning to face the room.

"You can call me Viv unless you piss me off, at which point you won't be calling me anything because you'll be as dead as Garth. All schedules will remain the same until I've had a chance to review them. Any questions?"

Adri bit back the urge to speak. There would be time to sound out their new manager once the Alpha was no longer in the building. Now was not the time to draw any attention and they all knew it. Every fighters' eyes were trained on the floor as they stood waiting to be dismissed.

"Good. Carter, with me," Marco ordered.

It took Adri longer than it should have to realise it was his surname the Alpha had called. By the time he did, Marco was already striding toward Garth's old office without even checking he was following. How had he even known his surname? Adri sure as fuck hadn't told Rafe.

It wasn't until Jay pushed him gently that he realised he'd been frozen, rooted to the spot. *Fuck.* He couldn't risk angering the Lunettis. Who would look after Jay and all the rest if he was killed? Swallowing his anger, he used his shifter speed to dart after Marco. It meant he made it through the door just as the Alpha took his seat behind the old oak desk. It also meant he didn't notice Rafe's scent until it was too late to pull back. Glaring at the man who'd meddled when Adri had told him not to, he stalked forward and threw himself into the only available chair. *Fuck Rafe.* The doc could stand.

Marco raised an eyebrow but otherwise ignored his rudeness to push a sheaf of papers sitting on the desk toward him. "This is the record of your debt. It's been repaid in full. You're free to go," Marco said.

"What?" he asked, blinking in confusion.

"You don't owe me anything. You can leave," Marco repeated.

"What the fuck did you do?" Adri growled, rising to his feet to face Rafe.

The russet-haired bodyguard stepped closer at the move, hovering between him and Rafe with a low growl at the potential threat to his pack. Adri's eyes flicked to the man and assessed him. He wasn't quite as tall as the Alpha, but he wasn't far off. The wolf shifter was packed with muscle, but it was the wary calculation in his gaze that told Adri he needed to tread carefully. If he'd been facing him in the ring, he would've had the thrill of knowing he was facing a true challenge of his skills. In this context, with the telltale bulge of a weapon breaking the line of the bodyguard's suit and the even more powerful Alpha nearby, Adri knew he was outmatched.

Rafe, the asshole, honestly looked surprised by his aggression. As if Adri hadn't explicitly told him not to save him. As if Adri hadn't told him to get off and fuck off. Adri couldn't be bought and he didn't need fucking saving. He was the one doing the saving. And he was going to keep doing it. No way would he leave Jay and the others to face the ruthless wolf bitch in the other room alone.

Marco's voice broke the tense silence. "Rafe didn't ask for anything I wouldn't have done anyway. I would have stepped into this business years ago if there hadn't been other priorities for the pack. I reviewed your so-called debt personally. What little of it stood up to any scrutiny was long since repaid by the money you've been bringing in. You were Garth's top earner."

Why the fuck was the Alpha of the Lunettis reviewing his debt personally? Was Rafe really that desperate for him?

"What about the others?" Adri asked, turning back to face the Alpha.

"No one else is near repayment. They have to stay," Marco said.

"That's bullshit!"

"That's business." There was a warning in Marco's eyes that said he was done letting Adrien's disrespect slide.

Forcing a politeness he wasn't feeling into his tone, he held Marco's gaze as he spoke. "Write me a new contract, then. I want all my profit going to repay their debt."

"Adrien, no!" Rafe burst out.

Stalking over to the infuriating wolf, Adrien poked him in the sternum. Hard. "I *told* you I didn't need saving. I *told* you to stay the fuck out of it. You don't own me just because we fucked once. You don't get to tell me what to do. No one does."

Irritation crashed through him in a wave as he noticed Rafe waving off the bodyguard like he wasn't worried about Adri at all.

"That's not what I meant, sweetheart. Please, think about this more carefully. I only just healed you from two broken legs and so many bruised organs I lost count. You don't need to be here. You could be safe," Rafe pleaded, reaching up to cup Adri's jaw.

His body betrayed him and he almost leaned into that touch. Almost. Why was Rafe so damn hard to resist? And why did he have to go and break the little trust they had between them before Adri even got a taste of him?

"You're wrong. I do need to be here. And you need to stay

the fuck away unless someone needs a doctor," Adri said, turning away.

"Adrien, look at me," Rafe growled.

Adri ignored him.

"Will you sort a new contract? Please?" Adrien asked Marco, finally tilting his head in submission the tiniest amount in the hopes it would placate the Alpha into doing what he needed.

Marco's eyes flicked behind him to Rafe and a silent conversation seemed to pass between the two wolf shifters before he nodded. As if the doc should have any say in his future.

"If that's what you want."

"It is. Thank you."

A strong hand on his shoulder stopped him as he strode for the door. He didn't turn around. Couldn't. Because if he had to look at those soulful brown eyes one more time or drag that intoxicating scent into his lungs, he'd lose his nerve.

"I'm sorry your life led you to this place where you can't let someone help you, but I'm not sorry I did. I'll respect this boundary you're drawing, but I will always be here for you, Adrien. I will always come if you call. When you're ready to let your pain go, I will take it from you."

Adri swallowed hard. "You promise?" he whispered.

Rafe's voice was deep and certain. A promise that sunk under Adrien's skin and shone the soft moonlight of Rafe's healing power on all the lonely, dark places of his hurt soul.

"I swear it."

PROLOGUE: RAFE

Thirteen years later…

"I need you at the fight, Doc. Now."

Marco hung up before Rafe could ask what was going on, and more importantly, *who* exactly needed him. Was it his Adri? Raging fear had him racing out of the clinic without bothering to lock the doors. Luckily, his last patient had left an hour earlier. He'd just been cleaning up and restocking before he went home.

At least he didn't need to ask where he was going. He made a point to always know where the fights the Lunettis organised were happening ever since that night thirteen years ago when he'd watched his too-young mate walk away from him after telling Rafe that he didn't need saving and to stay the fuck away.

At the time, he'd thought for sure the jaguar shifter would come around. Cat shifters might not feel the drive to mate the same way a wolf did, but they felt *something*. Years had passed in the blink of an eye, and he'd only been called back to the fighting ring twice in all that time. Marco's manager,

Viviana, ran a much tighter ship than her predecessor, and it was rare for a shifter or a vampire to need his healing power even in such a violent occupation. Each time he'd returned, he'd worried it was Adri who'd been hurt. Adri almost dying. And each time, he wasn't sure whether to be relieved or frustrated when his elusive mate was nowhere to be found. Avoiding him.

Police lights flashed in the distance as he pulled up to the warehouse. The stench of fear from whoever had just left was overpowering. It took a lot to scare a shifter. This was bad.

A ragged cry left his lips as he stepped into the building and his greatest nightmare came true. Adri's jungle scent, his *mate's* scent, was thick and heavy enough to drown him. It wasn't the scent of arousal, frustration, or anger. No. This was blood. Pain. Suffering.

"Pull yourself together or he's going to be learning to write with his left hand, Doc." Marco's voice cut through his panic with Alpha steel, and Rafe snapped into professional mode.

Adri's whimper of pain had him striding toward the ring.

"I don't need him," the jaguar protested, voice weak.

Rafe ignored the words. He was done giving Adri space. Kneeling down beside his beautiful, broken mate, he fought to control his emotions as he took in the mangled mess of his arm.

"I told you I'll always be here for you. I've got you. Whether you want me to or not."

CHAPTER 1: ADRI

"Give me your pain, sweetheart."

"I'm not your sweetheart." Adri gritted his teeth to swallow back a rumbling growl as he resisted the urge to roll his hips up and shove his ridged cock further into Rafe's mouth.

There was a lot of pain to give, but the combination of the heavy bandaging on Adri's shoulder and the doc's healing power like liquid moonlight in his veins was keeping him from feeling it so long as he didn't tense up or move. Something that was almost impossible when a sexy-as-fuck, silver-fox of a wolf shifter was making it his mission to suck his soul out through his dick.

This was not supposed to happen.

Adri couldn't even remember how he'd ended up in Rafe's bed. Not a bed in the doc's clinic, either. His literal fucking bed. He could tell it was his bed because when he'd woken confused and hurting, Rafe's intoxicating scent suffusing the sheets, pillows, and everything else had reassured him he was safe. Even though he hadn't been in the same room as the doc in over a decade. Even though he didn't need or want anyone to save him.

He hadn't meant to challenge the doc as soon as he entered the room to check on him. He definitely hadn't meant to throw the covers off his naked body and tell him just how to make him feel better.

"You're thinking too hard," Rafe said, pulling off his cock to press whisper-soft kisses up his chest.

"I'm clearly not thinking hard enough. Why am I here?"

Rafe swore under his breath and pulled a blanket back over Adri before he had a chance to protest.

"I'm sorry, sweetheart. I shouldn't have done that when you only just woke up."

"Fuck that. You might be an old man, but I'm not a child. You don't need to coddle me."

"Do you remember what happened at the fight last night?"

Adri's brow furrowed as he searched his fuzzy memories —the fantastical artwork like he'd never seen before at the ring, facing off against the new wolf shifter fighter who went by Black Fang, and then ... Marco Lunetti stepping in with his Alpha command for some reason?

"Why haven't I healed already?"

"The other fighter turned feral. Your arm was holding on by a literal thread. You almost lost it."

He owed Rafe his arm? *Fuck.* Now that he was taking the time to look, the doc looked drawn and exhausted. Probably from expending his healing power to save Adri's limb. Rafe was the one who should be resting.

Adri's good hand shot out to grab Rafe's arm as he went to leave. "Where do you think you're going?"

"You need food. And rest."

"I need you to finish what you started," Adri snapped, annoyed at himself for his weakness but unable to concentrate on anything but the throbbing ache in his cock. He needed to come, and then he could get the fuck out of here. Even better if luring Rafe back to bed meant the doc caught up on some sleep after.

Rafe's nostrils flared, and he shook his head like he was trying to clear it before half-heartedly trying to pull away again.

Adri's eyes trailed down his lean, muscled body, landing on the distinctive bulge in the sexy doctor's slacks. "Looks like you need to finish as well."

"I thought you didn't do repeats," Rafe said, his voice carefully flat as he stared at the bedroom door like it contained the answers to the universe instead of meeting Adri's glare.

"Come on, Doc. Don't be like that."

"Are you planning to leave once you get off?"

"I need to get back to work."

"You need to *heal*. In bed. If you walk around with your arm in that state, the weight and gravity will undo all my efforts to reconnect the tissue."

Adri growled in frustration. "How long?"

Rafe placed a hand over his bandaged shoulder, eyes closing as the cool wash of his healing shifter magic sank into Adri's skin. "Three days."

"Fuck off! No way do I need to spend three days in bed."

"Another day in bed, and then two days not lifting anything or making any sudden movements. I want you here where I can keep an eye on you."

Adri rolled his eyes. "We all want things we can't have. I'm not staying a minute longer than I need to."

He had obligations back home—young fighters he needed to ensure were safe. Especially now. They'd be freaking out after what happened. The problem was that he had no idea if Rafe's demands were reasonable or not. Adri had ended up adopted by his human dad's sister as a baby when his parents died. Jaguars were notorious loners, and his mum's family, if she even had any, had never come looking for him. Thanks to the Supernatural Council's strict rules about exposing their kind, his aunt and uncle had been oblivious to their sister-in-law's shifter nature. They'd raised him as their own, but he'd grown up knowing nothing of the rest of the supernatural world until he was kidnapped and trafficked by the Cruor Coven at eighteen.

If it weren't for the whole indentured cage-fighting thing, he almost would've been grateful to discover he wasn't alone in the supernatural world. All that meant he'd never seen an injury like the one he'd sustained, and he didn't have the benefit of growing up in a shifter family to know what was normal in terms of healing. He had no idea how much he'd be risking if he left.

"What will it take to get you to rest for once?" Rafe asked, his eyes flashing gold with frustration.

Adri reached out to grab his jaw, forcing the older man to look at him. "I'm sure you can figure something out."

Rafe huffed a laugh. "If you're a good kitten and eat your lunch, I'll think about it."

Fuck that. As soon as Rafe disappeared down the hallway to deliver on his promise of food, Adri turned onto his good side and dragged himself upright and out of bed. Black spots floated across his vision as he stood swaying against a tide of *wrong* radiating from his abused shoulder joint. His forearm and fingers appeared normal at a glance, but they were void of sensation, totally numb. He was sure that wouldn't last. He wanted to be back in his den before the full brunt of the pain bowled him over. His apartment wasn't much, not with how much money he poured into paying off the debts of his fellow fighters, but it was *his*.

He made it halfway to the dresser before the room tipped

sideways, and he found himself up close and personal with the wool carpet. Polished leather shoes filled his vision as he tried to figure out how to push himself back to his feet without twisting his body or using his right arm.

"Do I need to handcuff you to the bed?" Rafe growled from above him.

Nothing about the way Rafe picked Adri up off the ground hinted at the frustration he'd heard in his voice. A gentle hand stabilised his injured arm as Rafe lifted him from the floor like he weighed nothing before depositing him back on the bed, this time with a few extra pillows propping him more upright.

"I was going to let you feed yourself, but it looks like you decided to use all your strength falling over instead," Rafe said, moving to fetch something that smelled divine from the hallway.

Adri winced. "I can manage."

Rafe ignored him, scooping up a forkful of salmon and rice and holding it to his lips. "Let me take care of you. Please."

Too tired and sore to keep fighting, Adri opened his mouth and let the doc feed him. It didn't mean anything. And that definitely wasn't a purr of contentment rumbling in his chest.

Adri jerked awake to the sound of raised voices from somewhere below. Night had fallen, but he had no idea how long he'd been out. Adrenaline surged through him at the thought of someone getting aggressive with Rafe. No way was that fucking happening.

The food and sleep had helped, because this time when he

hauled himself upright, he only swayed for a moment before staggering his way across the room. He was still naked, but he didn't have time to stop and find something to wear. Rafe needed him.

Prowling like the jaguar that lived hidden inside him, he slipped down the stairs, pausing in the shadows just before the open door that led to the waiting room of Rafe's clinic.

"This is the third time this month, Doc! I know you know more than you're telling me. Let me take care of it." The Lunetti Pack Alpha's voice was deep and commanding, tinged with a growl of frustration.

"I deal with a lot of vulnerable, upset people, Marco. This isn't pack business. I've got it covered," Rafe replied, voice calm.

Adri could hear a rustling of movement, like the doc was moving supplies around as they talked. What was going on? Everyone knew Rafe's loyalties lay with the Lunetti mafia family. Why was he refusing his Alpha?

"Carter, stop lurking in hallways when you're injured! Get your ass in here," Marco called to Adri, making him flinch. Dammit. Of course, the Alpha shifter had sensed his presence.

A low growl left Rafe's mouth the second Adri stepped into the well-lit room. The doc became a blur of motion as he grabbed a towel and shoved it at him. Adri was too distracted by the mess of his clinic to respond. Someone had trashed the place. Wooden chairs lay in splinters, medical supplies were scattered everywhere, and the door to his examination room hung off its hinges.

"What the fuck happened here?" Adri snapped.

"Put the damn towel on before I lose my shit, kitten," Rafe shot back.

Adri's head jerked toward the doc in surprise, and he finally noticed how his eyes glowed gold as his fangs lengthened. Rafe's eyes dropped to Adri's exposed semi-hard cock and back up again, jaw clenched tight as his body blocked Marco's view of him.

Oh.

Adri's eyes narrowed as he grabbed the towel and wrapped it around his waist. It wasn't his fault adrenaline got him going, especially with Rafe's enticing scent permeating the space.

"I thought shifters didn't care about nakedness, especially doctors."

Marco was smirking from where he leaned back against the wall, watching them. "I'm not going to touch what's yours, Doc," he told Rafe.

Adri snarled, attempting to lunge forward to get in Marco's face and tell him he didn't belong to anyone but himself, but Rafe was right there blocking his way before he could take a step.

"If you damage your arm again in a pissing contest with an Alpha, I'm going to be very disappointed, kitten."

Adri swallowed hard, a hint of guilt slipping in. Rafe still looked exhausted. The last thing the doc needed was to expend more energy patching him up again.

"Fine. Who trashed your office?" he asked Rafe, mirroring Marco's position as he leaned back against the wall where the doc had caged him in.

"Not important. I'm old enough to take care of myself, as you so love to keep reminding me," Rafe said, moving away to grab a broom and continue cleaning up.

"Enough. You and Adrien both need to rest. We're moving this discussion upstairs. My people will clean this up," Marco said, typing out a quick message on his phone.

Rafe flashed the Alpha an annoyed look, but then his eyes met Adri's and he immediately dropped the broom to come wrap an arm around his waist.

"Come on, kitten. Marco's right. You need to sit down and eat some more."

Adri scowled up at the infuriating doctor. "Stop calling me that. And I'm not going back to bed."

"Didn't ask you to," Rafe replied.

"Wait 'til he's begging. It's more fun that way," Marco chimed in, moving past them to lead the way.

Adri's cock twitched, swelling even harder, and he almost lost the towel wrapped round his waist. His hand resting on Rafe's shoulder as the doctor helped him up the stairs flexed, gripping Rafe tight and sparking a sharp inhale in response.

Damn Marco for the image he'd just put in his head. How was he supposed to resist that?

CHAPTER 2: RAFE

If only begging would get Rafe what he wanted. Having his younger mate in his home—in his bed—without bonding him was an exercise in torture. When Adri had stepped into his waiting room wearing nothing at all, Rafe had almost choked on his own tongue as he took in the miles of sculpted fighter's muscles and resisted the urge to lick every inch of Adri's smooth, dark skin that was on display. The towel now barely covering him hadn't helped much.

"I'll find you some sweats," Rafe said as they made it upstairs.

Adri's smirk in response just about undid him. "You'll have to help me put them on."

Rafe huffed a breath. "Brat. Get in the bedroom."

Rafe tracked Adri's movement ahead of him as they walked down the hallway. It might've looked normal for a human, but he could tell the injury was affecting his mate. Cat shifters were usually all sinuous grace, barely making a sound as they walked. Adri was still graceful, but his cautious, padding steps betrayed the care he was taking not to jolt his shoulder as he moved.

"Do you need a painkiller?" Rafe asked.

He'd been maintaining a pain-block on Adri with his power, but it was possible some was still seeping through, given how tired he was.

Adri glanced over his shoulder, head quirked in question. "Did you forget I'm a shifter? They won't do me any good."

Adri's knowledge gap was another reminder that the jaguar shifter hadn't grown up in the shifter world. Rafe had caved and done a background check on his mate when they first met, outraged that Adri's family hadn't come looking for him when he'd ended up forced into the illegal fighting ring. That's how he knew Adri had been raised by humans who'd paid the price for fighting back when the coven stole him from his home. He hadn't been able to find any other living relatives. If Rafe hadn't already been determined to be Adri's family, that would've done it. Jaguars might be loners in the wild, but that didn't mean Adri had to be alone in the world.

"I keep witch-magicked drugs on hand for injured shifters. They're in a warded case, so they weren't touched when the clinic was vandalised."

"And who exactly vandalised the clinic? You forgot to mention," Adri said, turning to face him as he reached the drawers in Rafe's bedroom.

"It doesn't matter," Rafe said, reaching past him to find the promised clothes.

Adri caught him by surprise, reaching out to grip his jaw hard and drag his face round to look down at him.

"Yes, it fucking does."

Rafe pulled away, dropping to his knees with the sweatpants in hand and tilting his head up to look at his mate.

"Rest your good hand on my shoulder so you don't overbalance," he said, reaching out to help him into the pants.

Adri swore, his eyes flashing a bright green as his jaguar showed through. Instead of bracing himself on Rafe's shoulder like he'd asked, Adri tugged at the towel around his waist, letting it drop to the floor. His mate's cock—ridged, hard and dripping with pre-cum—now swung in front of Rafe's face, taunting him. Close enough that all he'd have to do was let his long tongue flick out of his mouth, and he'd be able to lick the liquid off its tip. He wasn't about to give Marco a show, though. No matter how much his Alpha would enjoy it.

Tapping Adri's foot, he forced himself to look down and focus on only the task before him—getting his mate dressed. As he pulled the soft fabric up Adri's muscled legs, it took every inch of willpower he possessed to resist the siren's call waving in front of his face.

"Not going to lick me clean so I don't make a wet patch on them?" Adri teased.

Rafe rolled his eyes, smiling despite himself. Was that bratting or catting? Was there any difference? His jaguar was going to be more than a handful.

Marco was waiting for them in the kitchen when they emerged, leaning back on the counter as he sipped a cup of coffee.

"I figured you'd want to feed him yourself, so I didn't start dinner," Marco said.

Rafe tipped his head in thanks and headed to the fridge to grab the soup he'd prepared earlier, chucking some hastily assembled garlic bread in the oven as it heated.

"So, what did you actually stop by for?" Rafe asked Marco as he worked, keeping an eye on Adri as he went.

Adri must've tired himself out because he sank onto a chair to watch their exchange.

"I wanted to ask if you're aware of any medical intervention that could've caused Adrien's opponent to turn feral last night."

Rafe froze before turning to face Marco fully. He'd never

heard of such a thing. No one with any sense wanted to mess around with a feral shifter.

"You think someone did that to him on purpose?"

"We've had intel that the D-2S has been running some kind of medical experimentation. It's too much of a coincidence to think that such a public, unexpected episode followed immediately by a police raid isn't related."

A low rumbling growl filled the room from where Adri sat. "They're targeting my people?" he asked.

Rafe sighed and pinched the bridge of his nose. The last thing he needed was Adri having another reason to run off on him. His mate was far too protective of his fellow fighters.

"I'll look into it and see if the Council's medical archives mention anything useful. It would help if I had a body to examine," Rafe said.

"I can't help you there. Silas took him straight to the crematorium. We couldn't risk it spreading if he healed," Marco said.

"Next time, contain them so I can figure out if there's a cause."

Marco frowned. "I'm really hoping there's not a next time."

"Do you have anything else to go on?" Adri asked as Rafe and Marco joined him at the table with their food.

Marco shook his head. "Things have been a mess with the police raid and everything else. We've been too busy diverting attention so that the Council doesn't get involved. Luca hasn't had a chance to dig into the fighter's digital footprint to see if there's anything suspicious there. Did you know him well?"

Rafe did his best to focus on his food when every instinct in him was screaming to go pull his stressed mate into his lap and nuzzle into his throat.

"No, we hadn't trained together yet. He was pretty new to

the circuit. There were whispers he'd come from an unsanctioned fighting ring. He was having conversations with some of the younger guys that I didn't like. Ones that only took place in quiet corners of the locker room and stopped when I got close enough to hear," Adri said.

Marco scowled. "There's another fighting ring operating in the city, and you didn't tell me?" he snapped.

Rafe's fangs lengthened despite himself, and he placed his cutlery down before his whitening knuckles could give him away. He'd sat between his mate and his Alpha by instinct. He was glad he had now, because it meant he didn't have to give himself away by lunging between them.

"Chill, Doc. I can handle myself," Adri muttered.

A flush spread up Rafe's cheeks as he realised he'd been subvocalising a growl. "Sorry, Alpha," he said to Marco, baring his throat.

Marco stared at him, assessing. "Do Carter and I need to continue this conversation elsewhere?"

"No. I'm fine."

"See that you stay that way," Marco warned.

Rafe swallowed hard and forced himself to pick up his spoon and keep eating. He didn't think Adri had realised there was a potential mating bond between them yet. Cats could be pretty slow on the uptake that way. It wouldn't take long for him to notice if Rafe carried on the way he was, though, and he didn't want to scare the younger man off.

"All I had was rumour. No proof. And I figured your manager would tell you anything you need to know. I'm not there for the pack. I'm there for my fighters," Adri said, his green eyes flicking between them.

"Does Viviana know?" Marco asked.

Viviana was the wolf shifter Marco had put in charge when the Lunettis took over the ring at Rafe's request after the last time he'd had to patch Adri up over a decade earlier.

She was as loyal as they came, but she was also an alpha, so her first instinct would be to handle things herself.

Adri shrugged. "No clue. It's not the kind of thing the fighters would bring up with her. It would put a target on their back. Make it seem like they were angling to leave."

"If you hear anything more, you text me. Immediately," Marco ordered.

Adri stared at Marco, holding his gaze longer than any wolf would have. Damn cats and their independent streaks. If his mate pissed his Alpha off, things were going to get super awkward.

"Sure. Why not?" Adri said finally, before focussing on his food.

Marco exchanged a look with Rafe, one eyebrow raised and a smirk on his face. Rafe just shook his head. His Alpha had been telling him to lock Adri down for years, but it wasn't that simple. The jaguar had an independent streak a mile wide. When he'd ignored Adri's wishes and arranged for Marco to take over the fighting ring he'd been indentured to, it had soured Adri to whatever was between them. Adri thought Rafe had a saviour complex. That he wanted to fix everything in his life. He wasn't wrong.

This time together was Rafe's chance to try to show the jaguar shifter that this need he had to care for his mate didn't mean he respected Adri any less or that he wanted to control him. Especially now his mate was in his thirties—not a young man anymore, but still some forty-five years Rafe's junior. Their hook-up when Adri was only twenty had been hot as hell, but even if Adri had wanted something more at the time, Rafe wouldn't have bonded with him so young. Had he left it too long now and missed his chance?

Adri's voice interrupted his spiralling thoughts. "I could go check out the unsanctioned ring if you want. I'm sure I can get one of the guys to give me the details."

"No! Absolutely not!" Rafe snapped before Marco could answer.

What was Adri thinking? He might be too out of it to realise, but Rafe was still channelling healing magic into him in a constant stream to manage the pain of his healing limb. Rafe had cancelled all his nonessential appointments, his energy levels running on empty as he poured everything into keeping his mate comfortable. And now Adri wanted to go undercover in an unsanctioned ring that might be run by anti-supernatural terrorists who were experimenting on their fighters?

If he thought he'd seen Adri angry before, it was nothing compared to the snarl his mate turned on him now. The draw on Rafe's pain-blocker grew as Adri twisted in his seat to bare sharpened fangs at him, his eyes flashing a brighter green and his pupils turning to vertical slits as his jaguar came forward.

"Fuck you, Doc. I'm out," he hissed, pushing to his feet and stalking for the stairs.

"Wait. You can't go. I can't hold the healing on you if you leave the building."

Rafe's heart raced in panic as he watched Adri walk away.

"I can do whatever the fuck I want," Adri snapped.

Wincing to himself, Rafe stopped all the power he'd been channelling into his mate, feeling like a total asshole. It would've cut off when Adri left the clinic and outside his range anyway, though, and it was far better that happened here in the safety of his home than outside, where Adri would be vulnerable.

Adri yelped as pain seared through him, and Rafe crossed the room in a blur of motion to catch him as his legs gave out, reinstating the pain-blocker as he sank to the floor, cradling Adri in his arms. The effort it took to restart feeding Adri his healing energy meant he couldn't keep his feet, either.

Marco huffed, and his legs appeared in Rafe's peripheral

vision. "You're both a mess," he said, lifting Adri into his arms and carrying him to the bedroom.

Rafe rolled onto his hands and knees with a groan before staggering to his feet and shuffling after them. His Alpha was gentle as he deposited Adri on the sheets.

"Give the doc a break and *rest,*" Marco told the jaguar. "And *you,*" he added, turning to Rafe. "Stop draining yourself dry. He's a fighter. He can handle a little pain."

Rafe ignored him and moved to pull the blankets up over his mate.

Adri reached out to grip his wrist with his good hand, his words slurring with fatigue from the shock to his system. "Stop treating me like I'm fragile."

"Then keep your ass in bed until you're not," Rafe grumbled, using his healing power to nudge the jaguar into sleep before shepherding Marco from the room so he could turn off the lights.

"He's going to run again if you keep that up," Marco warned as Rafe walked him out.

"He's going to run regardless. Wolves run faster and longer. I'll catch him."

CHAPTER 3: ADRI

Adri blinked awake in confusion, all senses on alert until he remembered where he was. Taking stock of his body, he was relieved to find the weakness that had plagued him the day before was fading. Somewhere across the apartment, he could hear the soft sound of Rafe typing. The angle of the winter sun streaming through the window suggested it was mid-morning. He couldn't remember the last time he'd slept so much.

Rolling onto his side, he carefully levered himself to his feet, scowling as he realised there was still hardly any pain. If he concentrated hard, he could feel a pleasant thrum that felt like Rafe centred on his injured shoulder. The doc really needed to stop exhausting himself for him. As much as he was desperate for a shower, he needed to deal with Rafe first.

"I know you said you'd take all my pain, but this is ridiculous. Stop wasting your magic on me," Adri said, leaning in the doorway of Rafe's study.

The doc leaned back in his chair, his assessing eyes trailing up Adri's body as a fresh wave of tingling moonlit power washed through his body. "You're much better today. Let me check and rebandage the wound. Then you can take a bath if it's looking okay," Rafe said, ignoring Adri's provocation.

"And if it's not? You gonna give me another sponge bath, Doc?" Adri snapped. He'd been horrified when he realised the blood and sweat of his fight had been washed clean while he'd been out cold. Fine. He *should've* been horrified. The less he thought about why he hadn't been, the better.

Rafe stood up from behind his desk and walked closer, pausing just out of Adri's reach. "Only if you ask nicely, kitten."

"Fuck off," Adri snapped, spinning to leave the room only to find himself pushed chest-first into the wall, one of Rafe's big, strong hands gripping his collarbone to immobilise his injured shoulder as he pinned Adri in place.

A shiver of need rocked through him as Rafe pressed blunt teeth into the big muscle at the base of his neck on his good side, biting hard enough to bruise. He couldn't help but arch his back to try to rub his ass against the infuriating wolf behind him. Rafe wasn't having a bar of it, effortlessly holding him in such a way that denied him any friction below the waist, even as Rafe drove Adri wild with his warm breath blowing across his vulnerable throat.

"Behave. You can be as frustrated as you like, but I won't have you being rude," Rafe warned, voice low and rumbling as he nuzzled beneath Adri's ear.

Adri snarled in response, sharp fangs drawing blood as he bit his lip hard before he said something he regretted.

"Poor kitten. Want me to kiss it better?" Rafe asked.

Adri tried to shrug him off and immediately regretted it as he felt the still-regrowing tendons in his shoulder pull tight.

Rafe huffed a breath against his skin. "You just can't help yourself, can you? All that anger and hurt with nowhere to go. If I get you off, will your brain relax long enough to let me check your shoulder and get you clean?"

Adri thumped his forehead on the wall Rafe had shoved him against with a groan. All he could smell was Rafe. All he could feel was Rafe's lips and the heat of his body pressed in close.

"If you want me to stop, just say so. With proper words. Otherwise, I can't tell if you're just bratting at me," Rafe said.

Adri's jaw dropped, but before he could express his outrage at being called a brat *again*, Rafe's hand had slipped down from his shoulder. Fiery desire ran down his chest, following the path of Rafe's touch. Adri's moan rang through the quiet study embarrassingly loudly as the doc pushed the waistband of his sweats down.

And then the infuriating man *stopped*. With a growl of impatience, Adri grabbed Rafe's hand and pressed it to his aching cock.

"Perfect. I love when you tell me what you need," Rafe murmured, sparking a tingling warmth in Adri's chest that was subsumed by arousal as the doc quickly and efficiently started jerking him like he had an instruction manual for Adri's pleasure. The familiar thrum of Rafe's healing power in his body had grown stronger, magnifying every aroused sensation he was feeling.

Lost to everything but that touch, Adri tried to press back into Rafe's body again, a growl of frustration escaping him as the doc still refused to let him grind back against him with his ass.

"This isn't a reward, kitten," Rafe said, his voice strained as he twisted his grip over the head of Adri's cock, making him moan.

Wait. *What?*

"If you want to touch me, you need to earn it," Rafe added.

Adri snarled again. "Let me guess, by following orders and doing what you say?"

"By letting me take care of you. Just like you are right now," Rafe said, tightening his grip and making Adri's eyes roll back in his head as the doc's magic raced through his veins, demanding his release.

Dammit. He was going to come. Hard. Leaning his head back on Rafe's chest, his orgasm was ripped from him, painting the study wall with his cum as he lost all control and screamed Rafe's name.

"Good kitten," Rafe murmured, pressing a kiss to his temple and tucking his cock back in his sweats once he was done.

Adri rolled his head where it rested on Rafe's pec, blinking at him as he tried to get his brain to come back online. When he tried to move away from the wall, he blinked in confusion when he was momentarily trapped. He'd partially shifted his hand, and his claws were still embedded in the doorframe, having dug a long line of grooves down the wood. He was quiet while Rafe directed him to the bathroom, still processing as the bandage came off and a tingle of Rafe's power washed over his injured arm.

"This is healing well. We can leave the bandage off until after you bathe," Rafe said, directing Adri into the steaming tub he'd barely noticed being filled.

Adri glanced down at his shoulder as he lay back in the hot water, wincing at the way the skin still gaped open around the muscle there. Rafe was ghostly gentle with the washcloth as he helped bathe him. So gentle that it lulled Adri into staying in the calm, floaty headspace his orgasm had thrown him into for far longer than it should've.

"You don't need to do that," Adri murmured as Rafe ran the cloth down his leg to wash his feet.

"I want to. Give me this, kitten," he replied.

Adri's brow furrowed as he tried to make sense of everything that had just happened, and Rafe audibly sighed.

"I see your brain is switching back on," Rafe said, setting the cloth aside. "I'm going to clean up the study. Call me when you're ready to get out so I can help you up."

Adri's face flushed with warmth as he remembered what Rafe needed to clean. Why had he let him do that? Why had he enjoyed it so much?

Ignoring Rafe's instructions, he got himself out of the bath not long after. It was a struggle to wrap a towel around himself one-handed, and he ignored the pink-tinged water dripping down his arm from his wound as he hunted down the infuriating doc. Thankfully, Rafe had finished wiping down the wall before Adri made it to him.

"Are you still hoping that same loophole applies from our first meeting, and I'll let you carry on doing this if you don't come?" Adri asked. "Do you really think you can hold out?"

It was bothering him that their interaction had been so one-sided. He wasn't selfish like that. Rafe glanced over at him from where he was making two cups of tea, his brow furrowing in concern when he looked at Adri's shoulder.

"I told you back when we first met that I would always be here for you, and I meant it. I could hold out forever if it was what you needed. But that's not what you need, is it?"

Adri swallowed hard, passing Rafe a clean bandage for him to rewrap his wound. "Shut up."

Rafe's eyes flashed, and Adri yelped as pain flared from his nipple where the doc had just pinched it. Hard. His cock swelled against the towel. Apparently, Rafe had meant it when he said not to be rude.

"Behave," Rafe said. "Or don't. I like you either way, but you might not be ready for what that attitude is going to get you."

"A bandaged shoulder and brunch in bed?" Adri snarked, sparking a peal of laughter from the doc.

It was the first time he'd seen Rafe smile since he'd been

there, and he didn't hate it. The doc needed more happiness in his life.

"I knew you'd be a quick learner."

"I'm not staying, Doc. I can't," Adri said.

"We'll see."

CHAPTER 4: RAFE

"Did you develop X-ray vision or something while I was gone, Doc?"

Rafe huffed in annoyance at being called out and dragged his eyes away from the wall where he'd been peering straight toward where the tug on his chest of the potential mate bond was pulling.

"Don't you have better things to do, Bella? You've been away for over a month. Go make love to your wife or something."

"My wife is plenty satisfied, Doc, and we were travelling together for the last week."

"I assume Marco sent you here to try and extract the information I didn't give him about the break-in."

Bella was his Alpha's best friend. An intimidating woman who smelled of fire and old magic. She'd never confirmed what kind of supernatural she was, but he had his suspicions that she was something out of legend, hiding in plain sight. She was also excellent company when she wasn't trying to intimidate you, and they'd been known to share a whiskey on occasion. He'd even met Katie, the wife she was so careful to keep away from the darkness of the pack's business. She was a medical professional as well, although she spent most of her time treating humans in the hospital.

"Can't an old friend stop by to say hi?" Bella asked, false innocence in her voice as her white teeth flashed in an aggressive grin.

Rafe ignored that and continued tidying up the kitchen. He'd been busier than usual in the clinic that morning, given he'd missed a day looking after Adri, and he hadn't cleared up from dinner the night before.

"Fine. If you're not going to tell me why your clinic still smells of angry young jackal shifter, you can at least tell me how your kitten's doing."

Rafe glared at the dangerous woman. "I mean it, Bella. Don't track them down. I have it under control."

Bella just stared at him, one elegant brow raised.

"He's a terrible patient, but his arm is no longer in danger of dropping off in a slight breeze," Rafe said, breaking the stalemate and hopefully distracting her by answering her question about Adri.

"You smell of him—intimately."

Yep, she was definitely not your run-of-the-mill shifter. Her senses were so much more acute than most of the pack's. He'd been careful to wash with scent-dampening soap before seeing any patients. Some of the people he treated had suffered trauma, and the last thing he wanted to do was trigger them with the smell of sex. Thankfully, he'd only had routine cases that morning, because even that mild use of his healing magic had wiped him out on top of what he was still doing for Adri.

Shifter healing magic was rare and worked differently from witch magic. He knew that because when he first realised he had the power, he'd tried to learn his craft from a witch. He'd almost burned out trying to do it their way before he found his own methods through experimentation. His healing magic was much more reliant on his own personal energy levels to manipulate his patients, working with their bodies to achieve the ends he wanted. Although the term *'healing magic'* was a bit misleading, a PR term at best, because he could equally use it for non-healing purposes.

"Don't let him hear you talking about that," Rafe warned, keeping his voice down as he felt his mate waking.

"Just take him somewhere safe and keep him there until he realises what he's ignoring between you," Bella offered.

Rafe huffed a laugh and shook his head as he went to make them a coffee. Was that how Bella had wooed her wife? "Safe? Or isolated? That's called kidnapping, Bella. It's generally frowned upon."

"I prefer hoarding. Most of what our pack gets up to is generally frowned upon."

"This is different. And not up for discussion," Rafe said.

They both turned towards the door as Adri joined them, and Rafe took the third cup he'd made over to his mate.

"How'd you know I take it with cream?" Adri asked.

Bella snickered. "Because you're a cat?"

Rafe shot her a warning glare. "Because I pay attention."

"There's nothing to be ashamed of in being feline," Bella said, her pupils flickering into slits and back. "Although you should really stop your kitten from clawing the walls like that."

Adri scowled as Bella jerked her chin to the marks he'd scored down the door to the study. Rafe probably should've grabbed a sander and buffed them out, but the marks made him hard every time he saw them. He liked the reminder.

"I'm not his anything," Adri snapped.

At least he was holding his temper better today. Bella had an even lower tolerance for rudeness than Rafe did, and he was too wiped out to go toe-to-toe with her if she took offence at something Adri said.

"If you think that, you're not paying enough attention," Bella said.

Fuck. She needed to back off.

"Thanks for stopping by. I need to care for my patient now," Rafe said, taking her still-full cup from her and gently shepherding her out the door, much to Bella's amusement.

"He just needs a little push," she murmured as they stepped outside Adri's hearing range.

"Any more pushing and you'll push him right out the door. He probably wouldn't come back," Rafe snapped.

Bella turned to face him, cocking her head. "He'll get there, Rafe. I can feel the draw between you."

"He's a cat. The only way he's going to get anywhere is if he chooses to go. He won't be pushed."

Bella smirked. "True. Reminds me of my wife. It's fun. You just need to find his version of catnip and then roll around in it with him."

Rafe sighed. "Go make trouble for her instead of me."

Bella's expression turned serious for a moment. "Make sure you take care of yourself as well as him, Doc. You're running on empty."

Rafe jerked his head in assent, watching until Bella's form disappeared down the street and around the corner before locking the door to the clinic and setting the alarm. The last thing he needed was another break-in while he was dealing with whatever Bella's teasing had sparked in his mate.

"Did you make me come with your magic yesterday?" Adri asked as soon as he got back upstairs.

Guess they were jumping right into it.

"I only amplified the sensations you were already feeling," Rafe said.

"Isn't it supposed to be a healing magic? Doesn't that breach some kind of oath or something?"

"I'm a mafia doctor, kitten, not a human one. I have a moral code, but I took no oath. I've definitely done harm before, although only to those who deserved it. How is using my power any different from using my hand? Did you not enjoy it?"

"I couldn't stop myself from coming."

"All you had to do was say stop, and I would have. You know that. You didn't want me to."

Adri growled. "I should have wanted you to."

"Why? You deserve to take what you need."

"I'm not an idiot, Doc. I wasn't *taking* a damn thing."

"You deserve to be given what you need, then. Would you like to know what else I can give you with my power?"

"No."

"You sure about that, kitten?"

"No."

Rafe smiled, stalking closer and taking Adri's empty mug from his hand to set it aside before caging him against the kitchen counter and running his nose up his throat as he drew in his mate's intoxicating jungle scent.

"I can make you orgasm over and over again without even touching you, totally dry while your cum swells in your balls, until your heart is racing and you can't remember a time you weren't bathed in pleasure, but every cell in your body is aching to feel my skin. I can touch you, suck on you, bite you, and shove my cock deep inside you, all while holding your orgasm back, controlling it, because I will *own* it. You'll be unable to come until I let you. Unable to do anything but take what I give until you beg me for what you need. It will hurt so good, kitten. You've never felt anything like it.

"And if you rile me up really good. If you're rude to me,

and brat at me, and storm out that door after you've given yourself to me, I'll make your blood head south, make you swell until you're hard and dripping, make your length tremble and throb, and then keep you that way. You'll be walking down the street, talking to your friends, training—and you won't be able to jerk yourself to release, no matter how hard you try. Won't be able to do anything to relieve the pressure until you return to me. Everyone who looks at you will know exactly who you belong to. Would you like that, kitten?"

"No," Adri said, glancing away.

The rich scent of his arousal flooded the room, and a quick glance down showed just how hard Rafe's words had made him.

"Liar. But don't worry, I won't do any of that until you ask. It's like Marco said—it's more fun when you beg."

"Never going to happen."

"Your loss. You're not ready for that yet, anyway. You still need to heal. Need to *rest*."

"So do *you*," Adri shot back. "I know you skipped breakfast. Sit down and eat something proper already."

Rafe's eyes softened, and he brushed a kiss over the stubble on Adri's cheek before heading over to the tray of food he'd left out for his mate to make them both a plate.

"I've got a fight scheduled for next week. I need to start training again," Adri said once they were sitting. He'd waited until Rafe had his mouth full so he couldn't immediately growl at him.

"No," Rafe said before he could control his instincts.

Adri froze, and Rafe knew he'd fucked up. Again.

"Thanks for everything, Doc. I got it from here," Adri said.

Rafe's knuckles whitened as Adri placed his fork down on

his plate with a soft clink before getting to his feet and heading toward the stairs.

"I can't maintain the pain block once you leave," Rafe reminded him, forcing himself to stay seated before he did any more damage to their fragile relationship by trying to save his mate from himself.

"Good. You shouldn't be maintaining it anyway. You're wasting your magic on me. It looks fine now. Any pain will be manageable," Adri said.

"You feeling any pain at all is too much," Rafe growled.

Adri huffed as he shoved his feet into his combat boots by the door. "I'm not a delicate kitten you need to protect."

"No. You're a vicious kitten I want to devour."

"Maybe try more devouring and less controlling next time."

Rafe relaxed a little. At least Adri was admitting there would be a next time.

CHAPTER 5: ADRI

It was only a short walk from Doc's clinic, just inside the neutral zone, to the facility where Adri and the other fighters lived and trained in Lunetti Pack territory. They'd moved there shortly after Marco took over the fighting ring from the previous asshole owner, and Adri had been furious at another example of how the doc's overprotectiveness had ruled his life. To Rafe's credit, though, he'd stayed away like Adri had asked.

Now, he was just grateful the proximity meant he didn't have to walk as far to get home. He'd been right that the pain wasn't too bad, but the dull, constant ache in his shoulder wasn't something he was used to with his shifter healing, and it only took a few minutes for him to be really fucking over it.

"Adri! You're okay!" Jay called as soon as he pushed through the door to the gym on the ground floor below his apartment.

He braced himself as a blur of colour headed in his direction before the vampire pulled him into a hug. Jay had been the first fighter Adri had used his earnings to repay the debt for, but he hadn't left like most of the others after him had.

Instead, he'd stuck around, watching Adri's back and helping him look out for the new crew constantly coming through. The ring had a high turnover that the manager, Viviana, encouraged. It kept things interesting for the punters and introduced a level of unknown to the bets on the fights that helped the pack rake in more profit.

Instead of working the indentured fighters to the bone like Garth had, the Lunetti Pack only kept them long enough to make a profit on their investment. They also had strict rules that had stopped the worst of the injuries. They weren't in the business of paying fighters to throw their fights, and they were quick to eject anyone who tried.

Was it annoying that the doc's high-handedness had improved things for him and the fighters he cared for like family? One hundred percent. That didn't mean he couldn't admit Marco was the best of all evils for them, though.

These days, with the fighters better able to repay their own debt under the new system, Adri spent more time coaching than in the ring. When he did fight, it was usually just exhibition matches when Viviana wanted to draw a particular crowd. Viviana's text to him that morning had made it clear the fight next week wasn't that. It was only scheduled to reassure the city that the pack had the situation under control after the shitshow of his last opponent turning feral.

"I'm fine, Jay. I texted to tell you that, remember?" Adri said, when the vampire's hug went on a little too long.

"You lost far too much blood," Jay chided, squeezing him one more time before releasing him. If anyone would know that, it would be a vamp.

"I'm okay. Doc patched me up," Adri said.

Jay's eyes sparkled. "Oh, really? Did he kiss it better, too?"

Adri rolled his eyes and shoved his friend's shoulder. "Shut up."

It was nice that Jay had grown in confidence since the young guy he used to look out for, but did he really have to rub Adri's nose in his own weakness?

"Carter, with me!" a sharp voice called from across the gym—Viviana.

Adri gave Jay an up-nod in farewell and sauntered as slow as he could get away with across the space, exchanging greetings with the fighters who were training as he went. Hopefully, his slow progress looked like he was antagonising Viviana rather than exhausted from the short walk here. Maybe Rafe had a point about still needing to heal. Whatever. It wasn't the first time he'd hidden a disadvantage from the other fighters. No one wanted to reveal a weakness to someone you might face in the ring.

Inhaling deeply, Adri let the familiar scent of the metallic tang of the weights cut through with the warmth of clean sweat and competitiveness soothe him. This was his life. His purpose—keeping the supernaturals who came and went from under this roof safe and healthy, so none of them would have to experience what he had when he'd been sold to Garth at the tender age of eighteen.

"What's up?" he asked the stern wolf shifter when he reached her.

Viviana jerked her head toward her office, and they headed up the stairs. One-way glass meant they could look out over the training fighters as they spoke without them seeing. It made him uncomfortable, but he knew it was a necessary protection in a gym full of people with inhuman eyesight who could easily read lips at that distance. Keeping the manager in his peripheral vision, he walked up to the glass and stared out at his people rather than sitting down in the chair opposite her desk, where she could feel like she was above him.

"Our Alpha called about the unsanctioned fight club you

told him about. Why didn't you come to me?" Viviana asked as soon as the door shut off all sound from outside. Her voice was clipped and angry.

Ah. He should've realised she'd be pissed about that.

"I don't have anything but hearsay and suspicion. You didn't ask. Marco did," Adri said.

"*Alpha,*" Viviana corrected him.

"He's your Alpha, not mine. Jaguars don't have Alphas."

"As long as you're working for the pack, you will address him with respect."

"He's not here, and I respect Marco plenty," Adri said.

Viviana growled, lunging at him too fast for him to side-step in his weakened condition and pinning him to the window by his throat.

"Your species isn't an excuse for your issues with authority. Don't test me, Carter," she said, snarling in his face.

Adri tried to shrug, immediately regretting it as it pulled his still-healing shoulder in the worst way. Viviana looked exasperated at him.

"Why did the doc let you out when you're still healing? I can't coddle you here."

"Didn't ask you to."

"You couldn't even listen to a doctor?" she asked, frustration in her tone.

"He's not the boss of me."

"Well, I am. Go take a nap, and don't you dare show your face in the gym again until you're strong enough that the others don't realise you're injured. We're trying to restore everyone's confidence, not break it."

Adri's brow furrowed. "I thought next week's fight was to reassure the city that things are fine?"

"It's to reassure *them,* too," Viviana said, gesturing out to the training fighters. "Casey quit last week. Sera was so tense sparring that she let Dray, of all people, get the drop on her."

Adri winced. Dray was one of their newest recruits, still too inexperienced to put in the ring. No way should any of their regulars have let him through their guard. "I'll talk to her."

"She's fine. This may surprise you, but it's my job to manage the fighters here, and I'm actually perfectly competent at it without your help."

Adri smirked at her. "You fucked her until she got out of her head, didn't you?"

"Piss off, Carter," Viviana said, pushing him toward the door. She was hiding a smile, though.

They might butt heads more often than not and come at things from different angles, but they both knew the other was essential to the success of the ring. They'd long since learned to work together.

The pain finally disappeared the next morning. Adri cautiously stretched in his bed, arching his back and reaching both arms above his head just like his jaguar would have if he'd let it free. It was tempting to shift and lie in the narrow line of sunlight cutting across his floor, but he should really get downstairs and check on his crew properly.

As he kicked the blankets off himself, he reached down to stroke his achingly hard dick, groaning as his fingers massaged the ridges ringing his shaft that were so much more noticeable and sensitive whenever Rafe was involved.

His dreams had been frustratingly commandeered by the doctor, images of all the things Rafe had offered him playing on repeat in his subconscious, leaving him uncharacteristically needy. Why did just the thought of the sensual torture Rafe described light him up like none of his hook-ups ever had? Adri hated being told what to do. He'd spent enough time with all his choices removed when he'd been captured as a teen. He didn't have any interest in going back to that. Nor did he need some knight in shining armour to whisk him away from the place he'd finally carved out for himself here. He was just fine on his own.

A firm knock on his door interrupted him before he could finish taking care of himself. Which of his protégés was bothering him before he'd even got out of bed? Groaning, he rolled out of bed and grabbed a towel to wrap around his waist, hoping the folds of fabric would hide the situation he had going on.

His mouth watered as the scent of fresh-roasted coffee and bacon washed over him when he opened the door. It took him far too long to process that it was being held by a certain salt-and-pepper-haired, sexy-as-fuck doctor whose pupils were dilating as he drew in deep breaths of Adri's scent with flaring nostrils.

"Mmm… looks like I timed my visit perfectly," Rafe said, stalking forward with his wolf flashing in his eyes.

Adri ignored the instinct to hold his ground, huffing in annoyance as he turned his back on Rafe to head to his kitchenette for some hydration.

"What are you doing here?" he snapped, tipping his head back to drink like he could trick his body into thinking that was the tall glass of water he was craving.

Rafe's eyes tracked his movements, the doc licking his lips as his focus narrowed on Adri's throat.

Visibly shaking himself out of whatever spell he'd fallen under, Rafe's voice was like gravel when he replied. "House call. I got us breakfast sandwiches from the deli down the road."

Adri forced himself to loosen his grip on the glass he was still holding before he cracked it, watching as the wolf shifter made himself at home, setting out their coffee and sandwiches on the tiny table pushed against the wall. His apartment wasn't big, but it had never felt quite so small as it did with Rafe's scent everywhere and his dominating presence filling the space.

"I'm fine. You don't need to check on me," Adri said, stalking to his bedroom to find some clothes that might hide the way his body was betraying him. Unfortunately, the sweats he usually wore in the gym weren't going to cut it.

He didn't need to look to feel the doc trailing after him. A warm hand gripped his arm before he could rifle through his drawers, trailing up to his shoulder in a tingling of moonlit power that made his heart race and his breath catch as Rafe gently investigated the joint.

"You need at least another day before you start doing weights with this," Rafe said, dipping his chin to nuzzle into Adri's neck.

"I said, I'm *fine*. I need to train."

Rafe's frustrated growl sent a low vibration through him where the doc was still pressed against his back. The tingling sensation of his power strengthened, coalescing around Adri's abused joint.

"Don't waste your power on me!" Adri snapped, even more annoyed.

"If you're going to fight, I'm going to make sure you can train safely. *Now* you're fine," Rafe said.

Adri spun around to bare his teeth at him, only to catch the doc around the waist as he swayed backwards from the harsh movement, fatigue visible on his face.

Huffing again, Adri scooped the bigger man up in his arms and dropped him onto his bed with a bounce.

"Take some of your own advice and rest, Doc."

Rafe blinked up at him. "Maybe just a few minutes."

Adri scowled at him, confiscating Rafe's phone so it couldn't disturb his sleep as he pulled out his own.

Adri: The doc needs a break. Can you send someone to watch the clinic for him?

Marco: Good work. On it. Look after him.

Adri rolled his eyes at the praise, chucking his phone on the counter so he could eat the sandwich Rafe had brought. He really needed to get downstairs, but the man in his bed was enticing his jaguar to stay. Leaning in the doorway, he watched Rafe's chest rise and fall with his breaths, all the tension and concentration gone from his face in sleep.

It didn't mean anything when he went to the couch and grabbed the softest blanket he owned, tucking it gently around Rafe's sleeping form. The one he shifted and curled up in when he was stressed, digging his claws in and pulling at the threads until it was just right. Just like it didn't mean anything when he closed the curtains so the morning light wouldn't wake him when it crossed the room. Or when he pressed the softest kiss to Rafe's elegant cheekbone.

"So good to me. Thank you, kitten," Rafe whispered before he could pull away.

He wanted to tell the man invading his space to shut up, but Rafe's warning about rudeness made him pause despite himself.

"Don't get used to it," he said instead.

Rafe's mouth twitched in a smile as he rolled onto his side, drawing in a deep breath as he burrowed his face into the blanket that was drenched in Adri's scent and fell back to sleep.

Adri stood there for far longer than he should have, just silently watching him. What was it about this wolf that his jaguar wouldn't let him let go? He didn't know much about fated mates thanks to his upbringing, but everyone said jaguars were loners. And surely, Rafe wouldn't have left him alone for over a decade if there was a potential bond between them?

Their last words all those years ago played back in his memory as he drank in the sight of the man on his bed. He'd told Rafe to stay the fuck away unless someone needed a doctor. Rafe's reply had stunned him: *"I'm sorry your life led you to this place where you can't let someone help you, but I'm not sorry I did. I'll respect this boundary you're drawing, but I will always be here for you, Adrien. I will always come if you call. When you're ready to let your pain go, I will take it from you."*

No one would respect a boundary for that long if they wanted more, would they?

He would, his jaguar insisted.

CHAPTER 6: RAFE

Rafe blinked awake, achingly hard and momentarily disoriented as he tried to remember where he was. Confusion quickly gave way to cursing as he realised he'd slept five solid hours and was in danger of missing his afternoon clinic appointments.

When Adri had left the day before, he'd spent almost all night researching what could force a shifter to turn feral. He'd barely managed an hour's sleep before he'd been out to visit the dock workers at shift change in the dark, early hours of the morning. They couldn't come to his clinic in Lunetti territory without drawing the wrong kind of attention from their vampire bosses, and he had to time his visits to treat them for the few shifts supervised by someone who owed him a favour.

There had been a sharp increase in accidents at the docks recently, and he'd known it was going to be a rough morning when a harrowing scream had shredded the silence of the container he'd been working from. One of the cranes had failed, trapping a young vampire and crushing their lower body. Their co-workers, underfed and drawn by the blood, had struggled to get near without succumbing to bloodlust. Rafe had been forced to use his healing power not just to heal the poor thing, but to sedate the biological urges of the other workers to feast on them.

The breakfast sandwiches he'd brought to eat with Adri had been as much to restore his own energy levels as they were to satisfy his wolf's need to feed his mate. He should've known better than to use the last of his reserves getting Adri's shoulder to the point where he wouldn't have any discomfort using it. His wolf didn't give a fuck about minor things like conserving power, though. It just wanted to give their mate every single thing he needed and make sure he never felt any pain again. Even if his obsession was never reciprocated.

When he finally located his phone behind the sandwich Adri had left on the bedside table for him and saw the message from Marco, a thrill filled him and he sank back against the headboard. Maybe his feelings were reciprocated after all.

Alpha: Your kitten asked me to sort the clinic for you. Rocco is there with one of the witches from the MC who heals.

Checking his calendar, Rafe made sure none of the patients who'd booked would be uncomfortable with a witch treating them. Luckily, there was no one who'd have a problem with it. He flicked a quick thank you to Marco before ripping into the sandwich he hadn't had a chance to eat earlier.

With his hunger sated and his responsibilities taken care of, his thoughts turned to his mate. The tug in his chest that hadn't left him since he met Adri all those years ago was pulling him down to the gym on the ground floor. Of course, his mate would still be there even though he'd only just recovered.

Smiling to himself as he remembered the way Adri had tucked him in, he shrugged on his jacket and made his way downstairs. His gaze zeroed in on his beautiful mate as soon as he reached the threshold of the training space. Adri was barefoot and shirtless in the sparring ring, his muscles moving with feline fluidity as he prowled around his opponent—a young bear shifter who towered over Adri but lacked the dominant assuredness emanating from his jaguar.

"Again," Adri commanded, sparking an impressively fast blur of motion from the bear as they attacked.

Bears weren't known for their speed. Although jaguars weren't known for facing down opponents head-on like Adri was, either. They were ambush predators. That didn't stop Adri from twisting his body in a move that made the muscles of his torso flex as he redirected the attack away from himself and sent the other shifter hurtling to the ground.

Rafe winced in sympathy, but before the bear's head could bounce off the solid mats, Adri was there, catching him to cushion the worst of the impact. Rafe couldn't quite make out what Adri said to the bear who was panting on his back on the ground, but a short time later, his mate was reaching down to pull the other shifter to his feet and into a rough embrace before shoving the bear off toward the showers.

A low growl rumbled in Rafe's throat despite himself. It wasn't that he begrudged Adri the contact with his mentees. Rafe understood pack and the bonds that touch helped build, although the supposedly loner jaguar shifter probably wouldn't put it that way. It was just that Adri was half naked, his throat frustratingly bare of the mark Rafe wanted on it, and as Rafe stalked closer, he could barely smell himself on Adri. It was driving him crazy.

"The door's that way," Adri said, not even bothering to turn to him as he gestured in the other direction.

Rafe stalked after him, waiting until they were far enough away from the people still training that they wouldn't hear his low words.

"Kitten," Rafe said, letting the warning sound clear.

Adri's bratty dismissiveness was exactly the kind of rudeness he could make the jaguar love to be punished for. Adri should know better than to turn his back on a member of the Lunetti Pack. Rafe might only exist on the periphery of Marco's operations, but he was still pack. Appearances were important in their world.

Adri snapped his head around, baring his teeth at him. "Don't call me that," he hissed.

Rafe wasn't going to do any of the things he'd promised the other day without consent, but that didn't mean he was going to let Adri get away with whatever he was trying to pull by giving him the cold shoulder.

Raising his voice a little so the supernaturals training nearby would hear and know who his mate belonged to, Rafe met and held Adri's gaze. "Thank you for letting me stay, sweetheart. Sorry I slept so long."

Adri huffed in annoyance, knowing exactly what he was doing. "Whatever. Don't overdo it this afternoon," he growled back.

Rafe's mouth stretched in a slow smile as he realised the jaguar couldn't help but look out for him even when he was pissed off at Rafe for invading the gym. Moving slow enough that Adri could bat him away if he wanted, Rafe reached out a hand and clasped his neck, rubbing his thumb down his throat to refresh his scent. Adri's skin was hot and sweaty from his sparring, his jungle scent swirling in the air, and Rafe stepped closer without meaning to, letting his fingers drift down his pecs, petting him.

"Fucking wolves," Adri growled, rolling his eyes, but he

also leaned into the touch, a sound suspiciously like the start of a purr cutting off as he cleared his throat.

He looked like he might say more, but then his eyes flicked to the other fighters and his mouth snapped shut.

"Come to dinner with me," Rafe whispered, letting his hand drift even lower as he leaned in to nuzzle Adri's neck.

"Can't. I'm coaching a fight," Adri said, his eyes half-closed as the rumbling vibration in his chest grew louder.

Rafe's tongue slipped out, lapping at his skin. Salt and desire burst across his taste buds.

"Can I watch?" Rafe asked.

"Can I stop you?"

"Do you really need to ask me that? I stayed away for years because you asked."

"Let him come, Carter!" a voice shouted from the other side of the room.

"Yeah, stop giving the poor doc blue balls!" someone else called.

"Not what I meant, Sera! Get your mind out of the gutter!" the first voice called back.

Adri groaned and thumped his head on Rafe's collarbone. "Ignore them. I do."

Rafe pressed a finger to Adri's chin, tipping it up so the jaguar was looking at him. "Invite me to the damn fight, kitten."

"Fine. You can come."

Rafe raised an eyebrow, smirking.

"Not you, too. You're too old for that shit."

"And you're too young to be so jaded. I'll bring dinner at six. We can eat before we go. I'll bring one of the pack's SUVs," Rafe said.

"I'm perfectly capable of getting there on my own."

"It's not as satisfying, though, is it?" Rafe asked.

He didn't wait for Adri's reply before leaving. He'd

pushed his kitten enough for now. Through the reflection in the window, he watched his mate's gaze trained on his ass as he left. Adri might not feel the mating drive the same way, but he was definitely feeling something.

He'd planned to take over with his afternoon appointments once he got back to the clinic, but Rocco nudged him away and up the stairs with his air magic before he could do more than ask how they were getting on.

"Don't need you, Doc. You're still scraping the bottom of your magical barrel. Go rest and get your mojo back," Rocco said.

Rafe shook his head in annoyance at being pushed out of his own space, but at least the unexpected free time would give him another chance to trawl the medical archives for the information they needed. Settling down in bed with his laptop on his lap, Rafe dived into researching any mention or statistics on feral shifters.

Most of it he already knew, although it wasn't a speciality he'd developed. Feral shifters were rare, but there was a one-in-five chance that a bite from one would infect the victim and pass it on. Usually, there were enough warning signs that they could be contained before they turned and hurt someone. Feral shifters lost their humanity—an animal stuck in human form, scared and hyper-aggressive. A common, unproven assumption was that the condition was a magical, rather than physical, malady of some kind, given it interfered with the shift.

Early efforts to treat the condition had focussed on partnerships with witches through the Council. However, as the Cruor Coven's pharmaceutical company took off and proved the value of human technological advances to the supernatural community, some researchers were now looking to broaden their methods.

Following a trail of footnotes led him to one such study.

The researchers had been using MRI scans to establish which part of the brain the ferality affected. Already under pressure from the Council ethics committee because of the risk involved, they'd been shut down when one of their subjects got loose while being scanned and spread the condition to a lab assistant. Three scans before that had shown a consistent pattern of activity in one of the glands unique to shifters.

Rafe's instincts were screaming that this study was important in some way. Which was all very interesting, but didn't get him any closer to understanding exactly how one might trigger ferality in a shifter at a specific time and location, like had happened to Adri's opponent, let alone how to stop it. Given another decade and a team of specialists, he could probably figure out how to use some combination of magic, drugs, and technology to stimulate that section of the brain in the right way, but it would be beyond unethical to even attempt it. How had the D-2S managed it without anyone noticing?

Glancing at the clock, he realised he needed to get going if he was going to feed his mate before the fight. Now that he had a place to start, he could send Luca in the right direction to hunt through the city's records. Especially if they focussed on the period when the MRI study was shut down. Typing out an email that included the names of the relevant scientists, the date at which the study had come out, and notes of what to look out for, Rafe sent everything he had to the pack's hacker before heading to shower and change. Once he got back, he'd give Bella's wife a call as well. She was a brain surgeon at the local hospital, and might have some insight that he'd missed.

Rafe might not have seen Adri in over a decade, but he'd learned everything he could about him, nonetheless. He knew the jaguar shifter had a weak spot for a particular sushi restaurant that was a little too far away and too expensive for him to visit frequently. Viviana had told him Adri devoured it whenever she brought it in for celebrations at the gym, but never sought it out himself. His interest in the jaguar was the worst-kept secret in the pack, and they all tended to feed him bits of information like that.

Placing an order for all of Adri's favourites, Rafe dressed down in slacks that hugged his ass a little too well to be polite and a collared shirt he left several buttons open on. He wasn't above luring Adri closer with the sexual tension constantly thrumming between them, and he really hoped his jaguar might cave and let them play a little tonight.

The wool peacoat he grabbed before heading down to the pack SUV Marco left at the clinic for him to use would stand out at the gritty fight, but he wasn't about to pretend to be something he wasn't. There were certain expectations that came with his position with the Lunettis. The vehicle was also stocked with everything he could need in an emergency—a rolling pharmacy and field hospital. Hopefully, it wouldn't be needed.

He was right on time when he knocked on Adri's door, bags of food in hand. His jaguar's reaction when he opened it was worth the detour out of his way. Annoyance turned to surprise as Adri drew in a deep breath and smelled the food. For once, his kitten seemed lost for words. It didn't last long.

"How did you know that's my favourite?" he asked, eyes narrowed in suspicion.

"I pay attention."

"Stalker."

Rafe shook his head. "That's Rocco. I don't peer in your windows or follow you through town. I just make it my business to know how to please you. Are you going to let me tonight?"

A predatory thrill had his wolf perking up inside him as Adri's pupils dilated and his heartbeat sped up. The intoxicating perfume of his mate's arousal bloomed around them as Adri subtly shifted his weight, leaning closer. The moment was broken when Adri snatched the bag away from him, placing it on the coffee table nearby before heading to the kitchen to grab chopsticks, plates, and a bottle of whiskey.

Rafe unbuttoned his coat and placed it carefully folded over a chair as he tracked Adri's movements setting everything out on the table. His mate might be playing aloof, but choosing to eat in the living area rather than at the tiny dining table meant they'd either be pressed in close together on his small couch or sprawled out on the floor. Either option sparked a wealth of fantasies in his mind.

As Adri straightened from his task, Rafe reeled him in, gripping behind his neck to pull him close and nuzzle into his neck, reinforcing his scent. He was forced to jerk his head away as Adri snarled and snapped at him with lengthened fangs in response, but in typical cat fashion, his mate almost immediately changed tack to butt his head against Rafe's jaw instead.

Squeezing his fingers tighter, Rafe started kneading the muscles in Adri's neck, massaging out the ever-present tension there. Adri groaned in pleasure, relaxing as he leaned into Rafe's body. Desperate to draw out more of those noises, Rafe wrapped both arms around his mate, shifting his attention to his shoulders and working out each knot with firm strokes. Their position had their chests pressed together, and the vibration of Adri's involuntary purr against his heart was the sweetest reward for his efforts. Another moan escaped his mate as his hands dropped to his lower back to keep working him over.

Pausing when his hand reached the edge of Adri's T-shirt, Rafe ran his nose up the shell of his ear.

"This okay?" he asked, teasing up the fabric.

Adri huffed. "Yes. How did you turn me into a fucking kitten in less than five minutes?"

Rafe chuckled when his mate froze, clearly realising he'd accidentally used Rafe's nickname to describe himself.

"Not that kind of kitten, Doc," Adri snapped.

Rafe was still nuzzling into his neck, and Adri's warm skin brushed across his lips as he smiled.

"What time do you need to get to the fight?" Rafe asked, sliding his hand under Adri's T-shirt until he could brush his fingertips over the hot, taut skin of his back.

The vibrations of Adri's purring grew even louder.

"About half an hour. I'll help them set up and then run through a warm-up with the fighters."

"We should eat, then," Rafe said, using his touch on Adri's back to direct him toward the food before pulling him down between his legs on the floor.

"There's plenty of space. We don't need to sit on top of each other," Adri complained.

Rafe kept an arm wrapped around his waist as he reached out to grab the chopsticks and collect a piece of tuna. Adri grumbled under his breath when he held the morsel out to feed him.

"Open, kitten," Rafe ordered, making his mate turn rigid in his arms.

"I'm only doing this because I'm hungry," Adri said, snapping his teeth around the food.

Rafe smirked as he reached for a bite for himself. Adri easily could've picked up his own chopsticks and ignored him. Just like he could've moved out of his embrace. Cat shifters could be so contrary, but they also couldn't help but love to be indulged.

Neither of them spoke as the act of Rafe alternating feeding them both became almost meditative. He was just enough taller than Adri that the jaguar could nestle into his body perfectly when they sat like this. With his mate's shaved head, there was no danger of stray hairs in his food as he pressed his face in close. He couldn't resist the urge to nip at Adri's jaw as he chewed another mouthful. If only there were time to strip his shirt off him so he could nip at every enticing inch of his skin before they left and leave a trail of his scent across his mate's torso.

"Now who's a kitten? Are you going to chew my face off?" Adri joked.

"I told you I want to devour you," Rafe said, his voice rumbling low as he tried to keep himself in check. They didn't have time for all the things he wished they could do.

"Why?"

Rafe paused, tilting his head to the side as he pondered how much his mate could hear without being scared off. "Because you're mine."

"I was bought and sold once. I don't belong to anyone, and I never will again."

"I don't want to own you like that, kitten."

"What other type of ownership is there?"

"The type where I belong to you as much as you belong to me—*with* me. Would that be so bad?"

"You're a wolf. An *alpha* wolf. That's not how that works."

Rafe nipped at his ear in annoyance, sparking a yelp. "With all due respect, you didn't grow up with shifters, and none of the wolves you've trained with have grown up as part of a pack. Your experience of the supernatural world through your trainees and friends has only been with the outcasts and loners. You don't know what you're talking about. Are alpha shifters usually more dominant? Yes. Because we're stronger. More able to channel the shifter magic we all contain. Do you know why? It's so we can care for our pack, our chosen family. We're *protectors*. Providers."

"I don't need your protection."

"I didn't say you did. I said I need to provide it. If you decide to let me one day, that will be you taking care of me. Giving me what *I* need. A partnership."

"And if I wanted to leave? Do you expect me to believe you'd let me go when you're part of the fucking shifter mafia?"

"I'd make sure you never wanted to," Rafe promised.

Adri twisted in his lap, snapping at his face, fangs lengthened.

Rafe ignored the threat and reached up to cup his jaw, stroking his cheekbone with his thumb. "You're so beautiful like this—wild—letting shifter instinct and the magic running through your veins guide you."

Adri's head cocked in surprise, the murderous look in his eyes fading. "Why don't you ever try to overpower me when I threaten you?"

"You're a cat. You're going to lash out at me sometimes without provocation. It's part of your charm. If I'm lucky, it'll leave a mark," Rafe said, shifting his hips a little so Adri could feel just what effect his little outburst had.

What his mate hadn't yet understood was that his snippiness was just another demonstration that he was becoming more comfortable with Rafe. Not only had he let Rafe feed him and hold him, but he felt safe enough to relax into his truest self. Cat shifters didn't feel the potential bond the same way, but they felt *something*. They could get there eventually. It gave Rafe hope for the future. He wasn't going to risk scaring Adri away just as they were getting somewhere by pointing out what they could be, though.

"So you're fine if I claw and bite at you, but not if I'm rude?" Adri said, his brows furrowing in confusion.

Rafe smiled, brushing his fingers across Adri's forehead to smooth the lines away. "I'm fine with whatever you want or need, kitten. My point was only that rudeness will get a very particular response from me, so you should be sure that's what you want before you go that route."

Adri's tongue snuck out to lick his lips, and his eyes dropped to Rafe's mouth. "It's like magic the way I fall under your spell when you're near."

Rafe's fingers tightened on Adri's face as the scent of both their arousal grew stronger. "I swear I'm not using a drop of my power … but I could be. If you want."

CHAPTER 7: RAFE

Adri's mouth slipped open, and Rafe watched entranced as his mate's chest rose and fell in panting breaths.

"We don't have time."

Rafe let his hand drop to Adri's collarbone, tracing a finger along it and down the centre of his chest, letting just a touch of his affinity with the wild magic in his veins out to make his mate shiver.

"Do you want to play, kitten?" he asked, voice dropping into a growl.

Adri shoved into his body, overbalancing him onto the rug they were sitting on until he was sprawled on the floor beneath him. Unable to resist the temptation, Rafe grabbed Adri's hips and ground up into him, letting their hard cocks slide against each other as they both lost themselves in rutting for longer than they should have.

Adri let out a sound that was part hiss, part groan. "We're wearing too many clothes. I'm going to have an imprint of your zipper on my dick."

Rafe smirked and took pity on him, flipping them over so he was on top and taking the pressure off.

"Better?"

"No," Adri complained as he tried in vain to get some friction back.

"Do you want to come, kitten?"

"Fuck you. You know I do," Adri snapped.

It was Rafe's turn to groan, his fangs lengthening as he knew his eyes would be flashing gold. His kitten wanted to play, after all. Adri immediately realised what he'd done, freezing under him.

"I wasn't trying to be rude."

Rafe raised an eyebrow, and Adri looked away. "Weren't you?"

Leaning forward on all fours over his mate, Rafe shoved his hand under the waistband of Adri's sweatpants, taking his shaft in hand. "Tell me you want this, kitten."

"I already told you I do," Adri said, panting as he tried to arch his hips up into Rafe's grip, but unable to move because of his weight on his legs.

"Beg me for it."

Adri tipped his head back, probably in annoyance, but all Rafe's wolf could see was his mate baring his neck in submission. His hips jerked forward in an aborted rut as he fought for control.

"Make me come," Adri finally growled.

Rafe waited, raising an eyebrow.

"For fuck's sake. *Please,*" Adri added.

Rafe tightened his grip on Adri's cock, gathering the precum leaking from his tip so he could stroke down his length, long and slow, before dragging back up again. "Are you sure that's what you want to beg for?"

"What the fuck else is there?"

"You could beg to touch me. Or beg me to punish you," Rafe said, licking a strip up his neck before blowing on it.

Adri shivered with need beneath him, squeezing his eyes closed. "Just do *something.* Anything. We're late. We need to go."

Rafe huffed another breath against his neck. So impatient.

Tugging Adri's shirt up to bare his ripped abs, Rafe sat back on his thighs to keep him pinned as he pulled the waistband of Adri's sweats down to reveal his steel-hard, leaking length to the room.

"Doc, hurry the fuck up!" Adri snarled when he stared too long.

Rafe's lips twitched in a smirk as he let his fingers shift to claws and traced one sharp tip down his length. "I won't leave you like this at work this time. Not with so much at stake. But I told you if you wanted to touch me, you had to earn it, and you're still being rude, kitten. So, no touch for you. You know what you need to do if you want that to change."

Violence shone in Adri's eyes. "What? You said you'd—"

Before Adri could finish the thought, Rafe leaned down to pin his wrists to the floor and reached for his power, using it to flood pleasure into Adri's balls. A sharp cry left Adri's mouth as his back bowed and his cock jerked into empty air before shooting stripes of cum up his chest, untouched, with none of the build-up it would normally take to orgasm. It was instant and intense, but Rafe knew from experience it would also be ultimately unsatisfying because of that. It would leave him needy and wanting.

A whine left Adri's mouth as his hips continued to try and jerk up against Rafe's weight holding him down.

"Shhh, kitten. You were so good for me, coming like that."

"Rafe," Adri complained, voice soft. "I need."

It was the first time he'd used Rafe's name while they were intimate, and the aching desire in his chest became overwhelming as he looked down at his mate, but they didn't have time for anything more. This had punished him as much as Adri. He'd just have to hope his ornery mate let them have what they both wanted once the night was through.

Pressing a kiss to Adri's jaw, Rafe whispered he'd be right back before racing to grab a towel from the bathroom. Adri was still sprawled out on the floor, knees splayed and eyes closed when he returned. Gently wiping the cum from his skin, Rafe pressed a trail of kisses up his chest as he tugged Adri's clothes back into place. His own cock was so hard he was starting to feel light-headed, but that didn't matter. All that mattered was taking care of his mate. Helping Adri to sit up, he reached for the glass of water on the nearby table and supported Adri's neck as he helped him drink it.

He could see the moment the jaguar came back to himself because every muscle in his body tensed and his head jerked away.

"What's wrong, kitten?" Rafe asked.

Adri glared at him.

"I'll let you come properly next time," Rafe promised, testing whether his mate was ready to admit this thing between them wasn't going away.

"I don't give a fuck about that. *You* still haven't come. Are you just fucking playing with me? Do you even want me at all?"

Who knew his kitten had such sweetness in him? "Does this feel like I'm playing?" Rafe asked, grabbing Adri's hand and pressing it to his zipper where the fabric was damp from how much pre-cum he'd been leaking.

"Then why do you never take your own pleasure when we're together?"

"Because I need you to have zero doubt you want to give it to me, kitten."

Adri huffed and pushed himself to his feet, heading to the bathroom. "I need to wash the smell of sex off me, and then we need to leave."

Rafe wished he could follow suit, but he didn't have anything to change into, and the smell of sex wasn't coming out of these clothes without more time than they had to clean them. He wished he had Rocco's ability to hide scents with his magic, but his power didn't work that way. He'd just have to deal with every shifter around them knowing exactly what Adri was doing to him. At least everyone would know who he belonged to.

As soon as Adri stepped out of the bathroom clean and dressed, Rafe stepped in close, gripping his nape and rubbing his stubble up and down his sensitive neck while he slid his hands up the muscles of Adri's back and generally did everything he could to make sure the jaguar was bathed in his scent.

"Fucking hell. Why don't you just piss on me while you're at it?"

"Is that an option?"

Adri slammed him against the nearest wall, gripping his throat hard as he snarled in his face, and Rafe held his hands up in surrender. "That was a joke. For real. Water sports aren't my thing."

Adri huffed in annoyance and stepped away, heading to the entryway without bothering to check that Rafe was following. Smiling to himself, Rafe followed after his mate. Adri was totally warming to him. Otherwise, he would've been sporting claw marks and a concussion after a comment like that.

The location of the fighting ring that night was a closed-down nightclub partway into Cruor Coven territory. While the Lunettis had taken over running the fights over a decade ago, they hadn't tried to contain them to their own territory. There was more profit to be made by continuing to circulate the locations throughout the city.

They tended to make sure the vampire fighters were on the roster when they were in coven territory. That night's fight was Adri's six-foot-five vampire friend Jay versus a cougar shifter Rafe was unfamiliar with. It was rare to find a cougar in New Trinity, let alone the ring. They weren't an aggressive shifter type as a rule, which made the fighting circuit in the city known for its violent inhabitants an unusual choice. This one was female and sticking to the shadows behind the bar as she waited for their match to be called. Her face revealed nothing as she focussed her attention anywhere but at the gathered crowd of bloodthirsty viewers.

"Who is she? I haven't seen her before," Rafe said when Adri checked in with him for the third time as he leaned against a wall, sipping at a shifter-strength whiskey.

The way Adri had continually looked to him and checked in on him as he went about his responsibilities as unofficial assistant manager and coach had left Rafe a combination of hopeful and horny.

"Indigo. She goes by Inferno in the ring. She's another new one—a recruit rather than a debtor—but Viviana said she had solid references."

Rafe watched as she started her warm-up routine, stretching on the corner of the space Adri had taped out on the wooden floor. There was no cage this time, just a thin red line the fighters were expected to contain their violence to.

The fact that Indigo wasn't in debt explained why she hadn't been on Rafe's radar. He only kept track of those closest to Adri, and Adri focussed on the ones who needed his support to get their lives back under their own control.

"Who do you think will win?"

"Jay, no question. This is just a chance to test out her range and strength, so Viviana knows where to schedule her in the future."

"And a chance to reassure the punters that last week was an anomaly," Rafe pointed out.

Adri tilted his chin up in agreement, all his focus on the two fighters. With his mate distracted, Rafe indulged himself in drinking in the beautiful sight he made. Not just his peak-condition muscles bulging against his tight clothing, but the sexy way he took responsibility for those he worked with.

As he watched, a sudden flare of bright light lit Adri's face like a bonfire, throwing it into sharp relief. The agonising scream that followed just about pierced Rafe's eardrums. Spinning as one, the two of them turned toward the chaos as the sweet scent of burning flesh, cut through with an unusual tang of sulfur, blossomed in the air.

In the corner of the fighting ring where Indigo had been stretching, there was now a column of white-hot flame. Her screams cut off before they could take more than three racing steps toward her. Not because of the fire extinguisher someone nearby had managed to send shooting in her direction, but because whatever had caused her to immolate was consuming her body so quickly, there was already nothing left to make the sound.

Rafe sent a wave of healing power ahead of him as he sprinted closer, pouring it into her body like he had an endless supply as he dropped to his knees and skidded across the polished floor toward her still flaming body. A wall of solid muscle tackled him from the side before he could reach her, and he found himself pinned to the ground by his jaguar.

"It's too late, Rafe. Don't drain your power again when we don't know what else they'll throw at us."

Rafe was about to snap at his mate that he had to at least *try*, but the tear that fell from Adri's lashes onto his cheek drove home the truth of what his mate was saying. The truth he could feel from the power he'd bathed her burning corpse in. She was already gone.

Swearing under his breath, he reeled in what he could of his wasted magic. Adri was off him a moment later, sensing the change in his focus. As his mate took charge of the venue, co-opting fighters and guards to secure the space while punters raced toward the exits, Rafe shrugged off his jacket and used it to smother the last of the flames.

From nearby, he could hear the familiar voice of Silas—Marco's second—on the phone to the MC, presumably Blaze, asking for a fire witch to get there as soon as possible so they could figure out what the fuck had happened. Rafe already knew this hadn't been elemental witch magic, though. Their powers might work differently, but it was similar enough that he could sense its presence, especially in a shifter body. This was something else entirely.

"What are you thinking, Doc?" Silas asked when he was off the phone.

"Bring what's left of her back to my clinic, and I'll see what I can figure out."

Silas jerked his head in assent before heading to the exit, presumably to meet whoever from the MC the rumbling engines outside belonged to. Adri stepped into his field of vision a moment later.

"I'm taking Jay home. I need to be there for him and the others," he said.

Rafe frowned, instinct screaming at him to keep his mate

close. To protect him. Viviana or Silas would order Adri to stay with him if he asked.

"You're not safe there. None of you are."

"Here's your chance to show me you're not trying to control me. I'm not a delicate kitten you can keep locked away, Rafe."

It took everything he had to watch Adri walk away.

CHAPTER 8: ADRI

Adri wasn't surprised to find several of the fighters with no debt had packed up and left by the time they returned to the living quarters above the gym. Word travelled fast in their networks, and two gruesome, unexplained deaths like they'd seen in the last week were too much risk even for people in their line of work. Of more concern was that a couple of the indebted fighters had also run off. Marco might be fairer than the previous owners had been, but he had no tolerance for disloyalty.

"Go and bring them back before Viviana has to officially notice. I'm fine," Jay said, as Adri hovered in the doorway to the dorms that were on the floor between the gym and the small apartments the older fighters like Adri and Jay could afford to occupy.

As he was making his way back out onto the street to track down the errant fighters, voices raised in argument drifted down the stairs to the mezzanine where Viviana's office sat. It wasn't like her to forget to close it. Drifting closer, he used his natural stealth to slip silently up the stairs until he could hear what was going on.

"Can you explain how a human with a cell phone got into your fight tonight, then?" a waspish voice asked.

Fuck. That wasn't good.

"You can tell the Council we have it under control. They've been dealt with, Leah," Viviana replied.

"The pack was already on notice. My supervisor isn't going to be happy."

"Do they need to know?"

"Call Marco and get him here. He needs to explain himself."

"Sweetheart, come on. None of that. We can work this out between us. Woman to woman." Viviana's voice was flirtatious.

"I can't keep covering for you like this." The voice wasn't so waspish anymore. Instead, it was breathless.

Adri rolled his eyes and started backing away. Clearly, Viviana didn't need his help with whoever the Council rep was.

"Let me make it up to you."

The click of the door being pushed closed cut off any further words as the soundproofing kicked in. At least he knew he had some time before Viviana realised anyone was missing.

Needing to find them as soon as possible, Adri shrugged out of his clothes at the exit before shifting into his jaguar form. It took him a moment, not as smooth or practised as some of the others, because he didn't shift all that often. He didn't have a reason to. The scents that rolled over him from the street outside were overwhelming in this form, and he sneezed repeatedly before he got himself under control. Was it risky shifting in public with a council rep just upstairs? Sure. But there was a whole fucking city out there, and he needed to find the runaways fast.

They were cousins in their late teens—Garett and Finn.

Shifters, like most of their recruits after Marco took over. Pausing in the shadows, Adri forced his overstimulated senses to focus until he found the thread of their distinctive coyote scent that was tinged with the red liquorice they constantly chewed. It was fresh. They'd left out this back exit like he'd guessed, heading toward the bus stop. Keeping to the darkness, Adri bunched his muscles up, springing upward onto a nearby fire escape until he could pad his way across the low rooflines of this part of the city.

The kids were arguing when he found them, Finn tugging at Garret's arm and trying to get him to turn around. Like the ambush predator he was, Adri dropped down silently from above, landing between them and the bus stop they were aiming for, knowing his green eyes would be glittering in the darkness.

"Fuck! Adri, you scared the shit out of me," Finn snapped. Garret looked more wary. "We were just getting some fresh air. Weren't we, G?" the nervous teen added.

"Yeah, sure," Garret said.

Adri herded them back to the gym, not shifting back until they were inside. The only thing worse than humans spotting a jaguar prowling the streets would be a naked, muscled cage-fighter chasing after two teens who were pale with fear.

"We wouldn't have actually left," Finn whispered.

Adri sighed, pulling on his pants before wrapping an arm around each of them as he directed them back up to their rooms. "I can't keep you safe if I don't know where you are. We need to stick together."

"I know, man, but between what happened at the last two fights and the shifters going missing on the street, I don't think you can keep us safe at all," Garret said.

"Who's gone missing?" Adri asked, brow furrowing in concern.

"A couple of our old crew disappeared near the doc's place," Finn said, staring very intently at his feet.

Adri tilted his head in question, waiting for an explanation for the strange behaviour.

"And?"

"And they're thinking maybe he had something to do with it," Garret mumbled.

Adri swore under his breath. The ransacking of the clinic was starting to make more sense. He hadn't been able to think of a single reason why Rafe would be targeted when he provided free medical services to everyone in the area. Nervous energy buzzed under his skin as he vibrated with the need to check on Rafe and make sure the violent gang these two fighters used to run with wasn't going after him again as they spoke.

"Doc doesn't have anything to do with this. He's helping Marco fix it, for fuck's sake."

The twins looked at each other, a silent conversation he couldn't follow.

"Is he yours?" Garret asked.

"Why?"

"Because if he's yours, you should go to him. The crew is afraid. They're getting reckless."

"Reckless enough to do more than make a mess, even though he's with the Lunettis?"

Garret shrugged, looking away.

Adri hesitated, torn between his need to get to Rafe and his need to make sure the two teens didn't get themselves in any more trouble. Rafe was big and old enough to look after himself, especially with the pack behind him. The trouble was that he *hadn't* been looking after himself. He was exhausted. Weaker than he should be. Especially after the way he'd thrown his magic around at the fight. *Dammit.*

"Can I trust you two to stay put?"

"Yeah. Like I told G, we're not even fighting in the ring yet to get targeted by whoever's killing people. Going missing on the streets is probably preferable to whatever Marco would do to us for running."

They were too young for the harshest kind of lessons the pack doled out to those who betrayed them, but Adri wasn't going to point that out to them. The more afraid they were, the less likely they were to put themselves in danger by leaving. Pulling them into a hug, Adri held them close until they finally relaxed.

"We're family here. We don't run from trouble. We face it. Together. Jay and I have got your backs. Viviana too. We won't let anything happen to you, but you have to work with us."

"Sorry, Adri," they both whispered.

"Now go see if Jay needs a hand," Adri said, pushing them toward the common room.

"We can come with you if you need backup," Garret offered.

Adri tipped his chin in acknowledgement, but waved them off. "I've got it."

Not willing to take the time to find shoes and weapons, he ditched his pants to shift again as soon as he reached the exit. He needed the advantage of his animal's enhanced senses and fangs. At least it was late enough that there shouldn't be many people out, especially in this part of the city where so many supernaturals lived.

The cold, dark night was the perfect cover for his pitch-black fur. It was no trouble at all to slip back up onto the roof to make his way through the shadows above the buildings of the city towards his doctor. Satisfaction filled him as he leaped across alleyways and roads, his powerful muscles propelling him through the air to land silent and deadly on the other side. Why didn't he run like this more often?

Because we're not allowed to be seen in the city, he reminded his jaguar.

A silent snarl curled his lips as he finally reached the building across from the clinic and watched a group of five young men whispering and posturing as they gestured toward it. They smelled of jackal and desperation, and they were nervous because the lights were still on. His doctor was busy working instead of sleeping. Again.

Wishing he'd thought to take the time to grab his phone so he could warn Rafe, Adri stayed where he was, waiting to see which way their fear would fall. He wasn't without empathy for them if their people were missing, but if they so much as scratched his doctor, he would rend them into pieces.

"We're wasting time. We go in, we question him, we leave. Marco's busy elsewhere. As long as he doesn't call anyone, we'll be fine," one of the men snapped.

Pulling a balaclava down over his head, he drew a gun from the back of his pants, leaving Adri with no doubt what kind of questioning he was planning on. His jaguar lost it the second he saw the flash of the barrel. As the five men stalked across the road, he poised on the roof above, muscles bunching as he launched himself to pounce onto their leader.

He retained just enough control to wait until his claws slammed into the man's back before unleashing a thunderous roar that no one would mistake for anything but the wild jaguar he was. The men he'd ambushed immediately shifted into their jackal forms, clothes tearing and fangs bared as their barks filled the night. They were much smaller than him, but there were five of the fuckers. Unfortunately for them, he didn't play fair.

Dipping his head to the still stunned leader of their little group groaning beneath him, he unhinged his jaw and stretched his fangs wide around the guy's arrogant little skull, sparking a screech of fear as the man realised just how much trouble he was in. Damn jackals and their high-pitched noises. Give him a sexy, growly, silver-haired wolf any day. A flick of his long tail had the man's gun skittering across the road, away from his twitching fingers.

"Adri, I know you want to show off that very impressive bite of yours, but that's enough. Let the boy go."

Adri bit down a little harder, breaking through the skin of the attacker's scalp to touch his fangs to the bone beneath, sparking another even higher-pitched scream. The other four jackals were circling, wary, but not willing to risk him following through on his threat to crush the guy's skull.

"You did so good warning me, keeping me safe. Look at me, kitten. I'm fine. These pups can't hurt me," Rafe said, voice soft as he stepped closer.

Adri snarled and released the guy, snapping his teeth right in front of his face in warning as the young man scrambled back to his feet.

Movement flashed to his right—one of the jackals attempting a lunge.

"Stop!" Rafe snapped, pure alpha dominance rolling over all of them.

Adri snarled, tail lashing as he ignored Rafe's command to focus on the threat. The four jackals and their leader, who was still in human form, all dropped to their bellies, too young to resist. Pacing right up to his doctor, Adri butted his head into Rafe's stomach, shoving him further away from the young men who'd been trying to hurt him.

"Oh, kitten. You're so beautiful like this," Rafe whispered, reaching down to run his hand down Adri's neck and grip his scruff.

Adri's chest rumbled in a purr, and he leaned into Rafe's leg, twisting to lick a stripe up the doc's wrist with his rough tongue. Rafe chuckled before turning back to the jackal leader who'd managed to sit up and was clutching his head.

"Explain yourselves," Rafe ordered, that sexy alpha command still clear in his voice.

"The last two of our crew to visit you were never seen again. We want them back," the guy said.

"Why didn't you come to me and ask for help?" Rafe asked.

The guy looked uncomfortable. "We know you had something to do with it, and we're not the only ones coming for you. It's not a coincidence that they both went missing here."

Adri turned his glowing green eyes on the man, lowering his head and growling low as he let his fangs flash in the streetlights. How dare they suggest Rafe would do such a thing? His doc worked tirelessly to look after them and everyone else who couldn't afford proper care.

"I'm sure it's not a coincidence they were taken from here, but that doesn't mean I took them. I had nothing to do with their disappearance, as you would know if you thought past your fear for one second. I've known most of you since you were pups. I swear to you, the pack will look into this. Now get your asses out of here before my mate takes a bite out of them."

Adri twisted back to face Rafe, barely noticing as the jackals booked it.

Mate?

Rearing back onto his hind legs, he placed both front paws on Rafe's chest, his surprise emerging in the saw-like call rumbling from his lungs. The noise turned to a purr, and his eyes slipped closed as Rafe reached out to grasp his ruff again, his other hand scratching behind one of his ears. That shouldn't feel so good.

"Caught that little slip, did you? Come inside, kitten," Rafe said, laughing when his attempt to back up just had Adri walking on his hind legs to stay pressed in close. "I'm tired, and you're heavy, sweetheart."

Reluctantly, Adri dropped back down to all fours, twining his way around Rafe's legs as he moved them back into the clinic and locked the door behind them. The move was somewhat hampered by his head being level with Rafe's waist when he was standing, but he made it work.

His nose wrinkled in distaste as he passed the threshold of the building. The smell of death permeated the space—charcoaled cougar. Rafe must've been staying up late to examine the body. The sickly scent was enough to send Adri shifting back to his human form, where his nose wasn't quite so sensitive. Rising from a crouch, reality crashed into him like a brick thrown through a window as human sensitivities took over from jaguar instinct.

Rafe passed him a pair of clean sweats from the wicker basket in the corner without comment, sensing his change in mood.

"I need to call Luca about the missing shifters," Rafe said. "He's been looking into things for me, and I'm sure this has something to do with the experimentation we think the D-2S has been undertaking. My patients here at the clinic tend to be vulnerable, with no pack or family to look out for them. They're the perfect targets."

Adri could hear the rage and pain hidden in those words. It was enough to distract him from that word echoing on repeat in his brain—*mate*. "If not here, they would have found them somewhere else. You didn't fail them."

"I didn't save them either. But I will."

Adri huffed a breath in annoyance. Rafe already had dark circles under his eyes and was moving more slowly than usual. He needed to stop trying to save everyone else and look after *himself* for a moment. His doc needed a fucking minder. He didn't like that Rafe hadn't noticed the threat from the jackals until Adri jumped them, either. Or that they'd suggested others would be coming. Where was Rafe's security?

"Call Luca and then you're going to bed, where you should've been already," Adri growled.

Rafe looked up from his phone, mouth twitching up in a smile. "Is that right, kitten? How are you going to enforce that?"

"I'll drag you there myself." And then he'd keep watch over his doc as bodyguard, because the guy clearly wasn't capable of doing it.

It didn't mean they were in a relationship or anything. Adri just owed him. And he couldn't stand the thought of anything happening to the doc. No one else would take care of Rafe as well as he could.

Rafe's smile stretched even wider. "You know, the best way to make sure I stay in bed is to stay there with me."

Adri rolled his eyes. "Call the damn hacker," he said, moving to the clinic's kitchenette so he could grab one of the energy bars and a bottle of iced coffee that Rafe kept on hand for when he was busy. "And eat something," he added, pushing Rafe gently into a seat and placing the food in front of him.

"Why are you so reckless with your safety? You should've had Marco on those jackals the first time they broke in," Adri said once Rafe had finished updating Luca on what he was looking for.

Rafe stood and stretched his back, twisting and reaching in a way that distracted Adri enough that he had to take a moment to calm himself before following him when he headed upstairs to the apartment.

"They're just vulnerable kids doing their best to survive in a dangerous city. You, of all people, should understand."

"They're adults, and I'm more than a fucking trauma backstory."

Rafe spun to face him as they entered the apartment, backing him up against the nearest wall and cupping his jaw in a firm grip. "I meant you understand what it's like to be the one standing between a young person and a life they shouldn't have to live, kitten. You do the same thing every day with those fighters coming through your gym."

"Oh," Adri said, eyes flicking down.

"And they're not adults by shifter standards. They're only in their twenties. Still too young to know better."

Adri pulled away from Rafe's touch, glaring at him. "Is that why you wouldn't go further when we first met? I wasn't a *child*. I'd dealt with more than most in twenty years. I was plenty old enough to know better."

"I didn't go further because I wasn't going to settle for anything less than *everything*. Old enough to blow me in a gym isn't the same as old enough to commit to forever. Forever is a really long time."

"Oh, are we admitting that now? The thing you didn't mention for the last *thirteen years*?"

"You asked me to stay away from you, so I did. I'll always do what you ask. Just like I'll always come when you call."

"Because of this … potential … between us?"

"Because you're my mate."

"Not without a bond, I'm not. I might not know as much about shifters as someone raised with them, but I know that."

"You have always been my mate, and you always will be. Whether you ever let us bond or not, I'm yours."

Adri looked away, unable to maintain the intensity brought by the eye contact between them. "You need to rest."

If Rafe was disappointed by the change of subject, he didn't show it. "Okay, kitten. Take me to bed."

Adri paused awkwardly when they entered the bedroom; his need to care for Rafe only taking him so far. The doc turned to face him, reaching up to undo first one cufflink, then the other. Adri was enthralled. Why was that so sexy? Placing the cufflinks aside, Rafe started on his buttons, the movements a slow tease as he revealed the dusting of black-and-silver hair across his toned chest and stomach.

"Are you just going to stand there and watch, kitten?"

Adri swallowed hard, tearing his gaze away from Rafe to eye his escape route. The soft jingle of a buckle snapped his attention back to the doc as he undid his belt.

"I'm not going to let you bite me," Adri said. He'd meant to growl, but it was more of a whisper.

"Didn't ask you to, sweetheart. Not yet."

Unable to resist the temptation a second longer, Adri slunk closer to his obsession, kneeling to undo the laces of Rafe's shoes and slip them from his feet.

"You going to let me touch you this time?" Adri asked, staring up Rafe's body to find the doc's eyes flashing gold with his wolf above him. He kept his eyes trained on Rafe's face as he tugged the rest of his clothes off.

Rafe traced a soft touch down the curve of his ear, sparking a shiver that left him purring. Again. How did Rafe draw that noise from him so easily?

"If you stay the night with me."

Adri narrowed his eyes at the older man. He always had to push that little bit further. Not that Adri could bring himself to leave at this point.

"Lie down on the bed."

Rafe tilted his head, considering the request, before sitting down on the mattress and shuffling back until he was reclined on his elbows in the middle. Letting one knee fall sideways, Rafe wrapped a hand around his cock, stroking it as his eyes stayed focussed on Adri.

"Strip," Rafe growled.

"You're not in charge tonight, Doc."

Adri didn't know why he was fighting him on the order. One little shove of fabric and he'd be naked.

"Whatever you need, kitten. But right now, I need that ridged cock of yours that's leaking into my sweatpants over here."

Growling, Adri let his fingertips shift to claws and tore the clothing from his body. His mind cleared of anything but need as he put one knee up on the bed to crawl up Rafe's body until they were pressed close and his lips were hovering over the enticing dip of his collarbone. When Rafe reached out to touch them, Adri knocked his hand away.

"Mine," he said, wrapping his fist around both their shafts and groaning as Rafe's hips thrust up at the pressure, making the head of his cock drag along each of the ridges swelling on Adri's length.

The image they made pressed together as he stroked was obscene. Adri couldn't drag his eyes away as even his large fist struggled to stretch around their combined girth. Every time he let his thumb brush over their tips, Rafe let out a gasp that he was already addicted to.

"So good, kitten," Rafe groaned, touching a knuckle to his chin to tip his head up and taking his lips in a brutal kiss, their tongues battling for dominance.

The world spun as Rafe flipped them over, pinning Adri to the bed as his hard thrusts into Adri's grip grew desperate. Adri's other hand dropped to grip his ass tight, fingers digging in hard enough to bruise. *Fuck.* By the soft-blooming scent of blood, it had been hard enough to break the skin when he partially shifted and lost control. He couldn't help but knead Rafe's muscled ass cheek with his claws, sparking a choked howl of pleasure from the wolf shifter.

"Fuck, yes. Just like that. Come for me, kitten. Now."

Adri's eyes rolled back in his head as his orgasm sent him soaring. Rafe hadn't even used his magic to prompt it. All he'd had to do was use that sexy, commanding tone, and Adri had been a goner. He would've felt self-conscious if Rafe wasn't coming just as hard.

As Adri lay panting on the bed after, he felt his claws withdrawing from Rafe's skin as they shifted back, sparking a low hiss from the man.

"Sorry."

"Don't ever be sorry for losing control like that, kitten. It was so fucking hot. It's not like it will take longer than a few seconds to heal."

Adri grumbled in annoyance, sparking a laugh from Rafe.

"Awww, you want the marks to stick around longer, kitten?"

"Shut—" Adri remembered just in time to cut off the rude words before he could finish.

"So good for me," Rafe praised, pressing a kiss to the corner of his mouth and then biting down gently on his lip.

Adri flopped back on the bed as Rafe got up, heading toward the bathroom. This was such a huge mistake, but he couldn't bring himself to care. The doc returned moments later with a warm cloth, cleaning their combined cum off Adri's chest.

"Mmmm, we smell delicious together," Rafe said as he chucked the cloth in the direction of the laundry basket.

"Don't get any ideas," Adri warned.

Rafe just smiled and rejoined him in bed, tugging him into his arms until Adri's head was resting on his chest, his heartbeat slow and reassuring beneath his ear. It didn't take any time at all for it to lull him right off to sleep.

CHAPTER 9: ADRI

"You two look cosy."

Adri had shifted to his jaguar form and crouched protectively over Rafe's legs to snarl at whoever had invaded their space before he'd even processed that he was awake. He only cut off the growl when he belatedly recognised Marco's voice, but his fangs remained bared. Rafe sighed behind him, the covers rustling as he sat up.

"Shut the door and go make yourself a cup of coffee while we get dressed," Rafe said.

Marco stayed put, leaning against the frame as he stared Adri down. Quickly bored with the game, Adri flicked his tail and twisted to butt his head under Rafe's chin instead.

"He's cute when he lets his jaguar take control," Marco said, sparking a huff of complaint from Adri.

"He's cute all the time," Rafe replied.

And that was enough of that. Shifting back into his human form, Adri grabbed the pair of sweatpants Rafe offered him and tugged them on, ignoring both of the irritatingly alpha wolf shifters taking up all the air in the room. Marco didn't give an inch as Adri passed, forcing him to turn sideways to barely avoid brushing up against him.

Heading to the kitchen, Adri set about making him and Rafe coffee, sighing as he caved and grabbed a third cup for the Alpha who'd turned up uninvited.

"Thank you, kitten," Rafe murmured, wrapping his arms around him from behind and kissing the back of his neck.

Adri couldn't help but tilt his head, asking for more, and Rafe moaned softly in approval. Sharp teeth bit down on the big muscle at the base of his neck, squeezing hard enough to make him hiss as his blood flowed south.

"As hot as the pair of you are, don't get distracted. I did stop by for a reason."

Dammit. How had Rafe managed to make him forget the Alpha wolf shifter in the room? It's like his jaguar became utterly fixated whenever Rafe touched him.

Adri passed Rafe the coffees for him and Marco before grabbing his own and heading back toward the bedroom. He needed to find some clothes and get back to the gym.

"Where do you think you're going, Carter?" Marco asked.

Adri paused, glancing over at him. "Shower. I figured you two needed to talk."

"Stay."

Adri's eyes narrowed. He wasn't a damn dog. A firm hand gripped his nape before he could snap back with something he'd regret. "Easy, kitten. It's his nature to command. Please come sit and have coffee with us."

"Fine."

Pulling away from Rafe's too-tempting touch, Adri grabbed a chair and spun it so he could straddle it and lean his arms on the back. A moment later, a T-shirt landed on his shoulder.

"I think we'll all be able to concentrate better if you put

those muscles away," Rafe said, staring down a smirking Marco.

Adri leaned back, craning his head to look up at Rafe. He might've played the move up a bit, making sure to tense and twist his torso to put his abs on best display.

"Are you jealous, Doc?"

"No. My Alpha isn't going to make a move on my mate. He might scare you off when he asks to watch, though."

"You won't even notice me," Marco said, a teasing note in his voice Adri had never heard before.

Rafe scoffed and pushed the Alpha's coffee over to him. "You'd be trying to conduct proceedings before I so much as touched him. No, thank you. Go to a club if you want to play."

Marco smirked. "You know me too well."

"Because I've known you since you were too young to know those clubs even existed."

"Shall I start calling you old man like Carter does? And when shall I clear the pack lands for your bonding now that you seem to be admitting what's between you?"

"F—" Rafe's hand wrapped firmly around Adri's mouth, smothering his words before he could tell the Alpha where to shove it.

"Put the shirt on and drink your coffee, kitten."

Adri glared up at Rafe, eyes flashing. Rafe stared back, unfazed, and cocked an eyebrow. Fine. Maybe now that he'd taken a breath, he could realise how monumentally stupid it would be to tell Marco to fuck off. Didn't mean he had to like it. Tugging Rafe's hand away from his mouth, Adri pulled the shirt over his head.

Marco watched on with interest, opening his mouth to say something until Rafe gave a tiny shake of his head. Fucking wolves.

"Luca told me about your visitors last night," Marco said.

"I have it under control. They're not a threat. They're just young and scared."

"I can't stand by and let a gang attack a member of my pack."

"They didn't attack me. Adri didn't let them even reach the door. And they left as soon as I asked nicely."

Adri rolled his eyes. That was one way to put it. The fact that Rafe could use an alpha command on a bunch of jackals was nothing short of bizarre.

"I'm glad your mate is protecting you, but I can't tolerate their disrespect. And you can't rely on your power to make them submit. They'll be expecting it next time."

Adri looked at Rafe with new appreciation and no small amount of frustration. Just how much could he do with his shifter '*healing*' magic? And how did the man not know how to stop and let himself recover? He didn't need to be throwing more power around last night when Adri was there to protect him.

"If we find their missing friends, they'll be loyal to you forever. No violence necessary. We need to get to the bottom of that, anyway. They must've been taken by the D-2S for whatever experiments they're running," Rafe said.

"Did you find anything on the body from last night?" Marco asked.

"There wasn't much left of her to examine. The sulfur smell during her immolation suggests demon blood was involved in some way, but that doesn't help narrow things down because a determined human can do a lot with demon blood. It seems likely the blood was used as part of whatever set her alight. Maybe because they don't have access to a fire witch, or because the security made sneaking a witch in too difficult. That's assuming the immolation was purposeful and not an unintended side effect of something else, of course."

"Given how dramatic it was and the trouble it's got us in

with the Council, I'd say it's a solid theory that it was on purpose. Anything else?" Marco asked.

"Before I got distracted by the jackals, I'd just found a melted ball of plastic and metal in her remains. It could've been from her clothing or the venue, but it appeared to be coated in burnt brain matter, and it had an interesting residue pattern. I'll take a closer look when I get the chance, but I'm wondering if they're using some sort of neural chip located in one of the glands linked to ferality."

Adri shuddered at the thought of someone digging into his brain like that. "Seems like a lot of effort to go to just to make someone crazed."

"It doesn't take more than one feral shifter on the loose to cause a major problem for us with the Council in the age of social media," Marco pointed out.

"And again, it's a question of whether the result was purposeful or not. We don't have a good grasp of shifter brain anatomy and function compared to advances in human medical understanding. If this group has targeted research on a particular gland in the brain, they could've discovered any number of other functions and effects of manipulating it that aren't documented in the council archives. I need to check in with Katie and see if she knows more, given her speciality."

"Bella's not going to like her being involved," Marco warned.

"I'll be careful. We can chat by encrypted video call."

"Usually, I'd tell you not to risk even that, but we really need to make some headway on this. The council is becoming a major problem. They're threatening to send in observers."

Adri didn't know much about the Supernatural Council as he'd been raised by humans and worked exclusively for criminals for his adult life, but he could see why you might not want them looking over your shoulder while running an enterprise like the Lunettis did. He also knew that if vulnerable shifters in the city were disappearing, it was only a matter of time before someone at his gym was targeted. There was no fucking way he was going to let that happen.

"Let me go check out this unsanctioned ring," Adri said, repeating his offer from earlier in the week.

"Do I need to rub your nose in the dead body downstairs so you understand how dangerous that would be?" Rafe growled.

"I wasn't asking you, Doc."

Marco's cough breaking the silence sounded suspiciously like a laugh.

"Do you have *any* concern for your own safety?" Rafe asked, turning to glare at him.

"Do you? You're running a clinic in the poorest part of town, too far away from the pack lands for help to arrive in time if you need it, with no fucking video surveillance or guards. How long would it take someone to realise you were missing if they came for *you*?" Adri snapped.

"Don't change the subject. I can take care of myself, and no one else will help the people here if I don't," Rafe said.

"Yeah, Doc. I know. It's the same for me with the kids at the gym."

"It's not your job to take care of every fighter at the cost of living a life of your own."

"And yet we do it anyway, don't we?" Adri said.

"Carter, I'll get Luca to hook you up with discreet surveillance and have Angelo put some people on you for backup," Marco said, interrupting their stand-off.

"We weren't finished that conversation, Alpha!" Rafe snapped, his eyes turning gold with his wolf.

"Yes, you were. I understand your need to keep your mate safe. That's why I'll have people shadowing him. Do you trust me to look after my pack, Rafael?" There was a sharp edge of warning in Marco's voice as he focussed on the doc that had Adri's lips peeling back in a warning snarl.

"I'm not part of your pack," Adri said, leaning forward so he'd be ready to pounce between the men if needed.

The full force of Marco's gaze turned on him, and his jaguar hissed inside him at the wolf trying to dominate him. There was only one wolf in the world he would submit to, and it wasn't Marco Fucking Lunetti.

Wait. What? NO wolves. There were *no* wolves he'd submit to.

"Even if you hadn't worked for me for over a decade, you belong to Rafe; therefore, you're pack. Whether you like it or not," Marco said, turning back to the doc to continue their stare-off.

Rafe immediately tipped his head to the side, baring his throat, which only pissed Adri off more. His jaguar really didn't like the threat to their doc, and Adri couldn't resist the urge to lean over and rest his chin on Rafe's shoulder, putting his head between Rafe's vulnerable neck and the annoyed Alpha throwing his weight around.

The move broke the tension between them, but not in the way he'd meant to. The two older wolves shared a knowing smile that had Adri rolling his eyes and scooping up the empty coffee cups to take them to the sink before he said something that started everyone growling again. Fucking wolves.

"Apologies, Alpha. I know you, of all people, wouldn't put a mate bond at risk," Rafe said.

Adri wondered what the story behind that was. Why Marco, '*of all people*'? He'd have to ask Rafe later.

"If you claimed him, the risk would be less. A tracking device can be removed," Marco told Rafe.

Adri scoffed, sarcasm dripping in his words. "So romantic. Forming a mating bond for *eternity*, just for the convenience of being able to find me if someone happens to grab me. Definitely the best reason to make a permanent, life-altering decision."

"To be fair, I agree. That is quite far down my very long list of reasons you should let me bond you," Rafe said.

Adri's head whipped round to the doc. What the fuck? How long had he been sitting on this '*list*'? In thirteen years, Rafe had never even mentioned they were mates until the previous night. Now he had a fucking list?

"I'm more interested in what could possibly be on Carter's list of reasons why not," Marco said.

"How about because we haven't even spent an entire week in each other's company? Or because no one is *ever* going to fucking own me again, and I don't need a man to give my life meaning? Or because I'm not interested in some dominant wolf trying to tell me what to do forever?"

"Well, that last one's just an outright lie, kitten," Marco said.

"Alpha, with all due respect, I don't need you to have this conversation for me, and I *really* don't need you to call him that," Rafe said.

How had this conversation got so off track?

"I'll talk to my people this afternoon. See if I can get an invite to wherever they're training for this other ring," Adri said, dragging the conversation back where it was supposed to be.

"How are you going to convince them you're not just spying for me?" Marco asked.

Adri smirked. "They've heard me tell Viviana you're not *my* Alpha enough times. I'll have a loud conversation with Jay about how Rafe doesn't fucking own me, and I'm sick of the Lunettis thinking I'll ever be part of your pack."

Marco's eyes glittered dangerously, and Rafe got that

particular tension in his jaw that said he was not impressed with his rudeness.

Oops.

"I'll handle him, Alpha," Rafe said, pissing him off even more.

Adri leaned back against the wall and crossed his arms. A rookie mistake, and not something he would've done in the ring, because Rafe moved so fast across the room, Adri didn't have a chance to uncross them before the wolf had him pinned—one hand keeping his arms trapped, and the other wrapped round his throat.

As strong as Adri was, the older, larger wolf shifter was an immovable object against him as he shoved his thigh between Adri's legs. Adri scowled at the smug look on Rafe's face as his leg rubbed against Adri's arousal. It wasn't his fault that the way Rafe could take control of a space was so fucking sexy. Adri had spent years trying to embed that skill in the fighters he trained, and here was a damn doctor who could do it as easily as breathing.

Marco took his time getting to his feet before coming to stand near them. "Carter, Angelo will text you when your support is in place. Don't go anywhere with anyone until you have backup."

"This is when you say: '*Thank you, Alpha.*' Because he already explained that you *are* pack," Rafe warned.

Marco overruling Rafe on Adri's involvement had clearly left the doc cranky. Adri reminded himself he'd won the argument about checking out the fighting ring, even if the position he was in made it feel like maybe they'd been arguing about something else entirely. Turning his head as far as he could in Rafe's tight grip, Adri met Marco's eyes.

"Thank you, Marco." He'd be damned if he called him Alpha or dropped his gaze. Even if they were determined to tell him he was pack, he was not a fucking wolf.

"Why do cats always have to be so contrary? Good enough," Marco said, turning to leave.

"You have to stop challenging him, kitten," Rafe said as soon as Marco's presence had faded from his awareness, still pinning him to the wall.

"I'm not challenging him. I'm just not submitting because I have no interest in your hierarchy," Adri said.

"You don't have to find this fighting ring for him. We can do it some other way."

"I'm not doing it for him. I'm doing it for me, and for the fighters so scared they want to run. Do you really think anyone could make me do something I don't want to?"

"Does that mean you wanted to come on command last night?"

Adri groaned in frustration at the way his doc loved to twist a conversation in a direction he wasn't prepared for.

"I need to get back to the gym," Adri said instead of answering.

"Not until Angelo's people are here to shadow you. Answer the question, kitten."

"Of course I wanted to come."

"That's not what I asked."

"Don't ask questions you already know the answer to."

"But I want to hear you say it."

"You want me to tell you I won't submit to your Alpha, but I'll submit to you?"

Adri watched in fascination as Rafe's pupils dilated and his lengthening fangs flashed into view as he licked his lips. The hand pinning his arms tightened, but the one wrapped around his throat stayed gentle. Adri leaned into that grip harder, eyes half-lidded as the pressure of Rafe's strong fingers on his carotid increased.

"Fuck, you're so perfect for me, kitten."

"I didn't say it." Technically.

"Your body said it for you."

"Just as long as you don't go hearing things it's not saying. I'm not going to let you claim me."

"Ever?"

Rafe's grey eyes were deep enough to drown in as he stared into what felt like Adri's soul. It was too much. Closing his eyes, Adri twisted, huffing when he still couldn't get free. The grip on his throat loosened, and Rafe slid his hand to his nape, gripping firmly in a way that had his jaguar instantly relaxing inside him. The silence between them was heavy as Rafe stood there. Waiting. Just like he had been for the last thirteen years.

"You're the most patient wolf I've ever met."

Rafe smiled, leaning forward to nuzzle under his ear. "You're worth the wait, kitten. Besides, wolves are persistence hunters. I'll just keep running and running after you until you're ready to drop all those defences you keep so high."

A laugh burst from Adri's chest, and he tilted his head to let Rafe trail his kisses down his neck. "So, you're just going to wear me out until I give up?"

"Will that work?"

"I can think of more fun ways to wear me out."

"I'm willing to negotiate. I can be flexible like that."

Adri snorted. "You're the most deceptively dominant person I've ever met. Lulling everyone into a false sense of security with your whole '*I'm just a caring doctor*' routine. You could give Marco a run for his money with how much you want to take control."

"You love it."

"I'm not just going to roll over for you."

"I'd be disappointed if you did."

Adri opened his eyes, blinking against the light as Rafe's face came back into focus. "You really would, wouldn't you?"

"I told you, you're perfect for me. I don't want to change

you. I just don't want to give the world the slightest chance to break you."

"I don't break that easy, Doc."

"Everyone breaks easily," Rafe said, old pain in his eyes. "The reason I studied healing was because my best friend died in my arms, and there was nothing I could do to stop it. I lived through the last shifter wars when the pack lost most of a generation to weapons that never should've been allowed. I watched Marco step up to lead far too young, only to witness his mate gunned down in front of him less than two years later. We may heal faster. We may be able to live forever *in theory*, but we're still fragile. I know that better than anyone because I see it in my work every day. Deep down, we will always be as mortal as any human because we succumb to fear, and hate, and violence just like them."

Adri's eyes pricked with tears. There was so much pain in him. Such deep wounds he'd had no idea were there. It explained so much of Rafe's behaviour. His compulsion to heal Adri when he didn't have the power to spare, the way he tried to keep him from any danger, even when he knew it would piss him off. The knowledge cracked something open inside him.

Because he's our person, his jaguar said inside him, all casual like he should've already known.

"Humans aren't all bad. They can love, too. Their lives could end at any minute, and they need to seize each moment that they have," Adri said.

Rafe rested his head on Adri's collarbone, his body going lax as he let his hands slide down Adri's arms. "That's not how humans love, sweetheart, but it's how I would love you if you let me."

"Give me time," Adri whispered.

Rafe raised his head, searching his eyes. "Don't say something you don't mean to make me feel better. I don't need false hope."

Adri reached up to cup his jaw, leaning forward to press a soft kiss to his lips. The need to take some of Rafe's pain outweighed all his efforts to hold himself back. "No. You need real hope. Enough to balance out a lifetime of loss and guilt. I can give you that much. I'm not ready for you to claim me today or tomorrow, but I'm so fucking gone for you, Rafe. I have been since that night you got on your knees for me on the dirty changing room floor all those years ago."

"So, next week, then?" Rafe teased, sparking another laugh from him.

"I take it back. Least patient wolf ever."

Their moment was interrupted by an urgent patient at the clinic, and a string of messages Rafe needed to deal with that had him stuck downstairs. Adri used the time to make the overworked doctor a meal that would be easy to heat when he was ready, before slipping out the back entrance as soon as Angelo texted to tell him his bodyguards were there.

The two women who'd be shadowing him blended into the background despite the air of danger that came from their wolf sides. They quickly set him up with a tracker—a tiny dot pressed into his skin that they said would stay with him even if he shifted—along with a few spares he could use on the fighters he was targeting if he got the chance.

He was more grateful for their invisible presence than he thought he'd be when he returned to the gym. It was suspiciously easy to get a couple of the newer guys to bring him along with them to what they called a selection waiting point, where fighters could be picked up for the evening's entertainment wherever this unsanctioned ring was operating from. Either the ring was desperate for new fighters because they kept killing off the ones they had, or someone had identified

Adri as a problem and was luring him into a trap. He suspected the latter.

Confirming his theory, Axel and Bo—the two guys he'd targeted for this—seemed nervous as they led him through the city on foot. Their conversation was a stilted back and forth of the type of toxic masculinity fighter bullshit Adri didn't have time for. He wasn't worried about the guys jumping him. He'd seen them in action at the gym and knew he could take them both if needed. What he was worried about was how far into vampire territory this meeting point was. It was pinging all his jaguar's instincts. An ambush predator could sense when it was walking into one, and the dead-end alley overlooked by three storeys of dark windows he couldn't see into was the last place he would've chosen to linger.

"Do you always meet here? How many fights have you done with these people?" Adri asked, his nose wrinkling at the smell of old garbage and spilled alcohol—smells that were strong enough to hide anyone's approach.

Axel glanced back at him. "Having second thoughts, Crusher?"

Before he could answer, they reached a grimy metal door, and Axel raised his fist to knock on it. A skittering noise from behind them had Adri turning away to search the shadows of the alley for any threat as the door's hinges squeaked in complaint at their use. Shifting his eyes so he could see better in the darkness, Adri scanned his surroundings, wondering how far back Angelo's guards had waited to stay out of sight.

A loud crash startled him into jumping to put his back to the wall. The door had slammed shut behind the two men he'd been following, leaving him alone on this side. Swearing to himself, Adri didn't hesitate, sprinting back toward the road. Metal flashed from a window overhead, and he shifted mid-stride as the concrete where his head had been a moment earlier exploded in a burst of gunfire. Pain and a sharp impact in his shoulder had him staggering when he landed on four paws, but a flash of movement ahead showed Angelo's people had finally joined the fray.

Leaping up onto the nearest fire escape, Adri pounced before the figure taking potshots could get another one off, squeezing his teeth around their skull and using his grip to throw them into the alleyway below. If the attacker was human, they probably hadn't survived the rag doll treatment of being thrown that way. Too bad. Adri wasn't fucking playing. Angelo's guards could scrape whoever it was up off the ground.

Ignoring the blood oozing from his aching shoulder—the same one he'd almost lost to the feral fighter the other day—Adri carried on scaling the fire escape up to the roofline that was his own personal highway in the city. Padding on silent feet, he stalked across the building, nose twitching as he drew in deep breaths of air, searching for the scent of the two men he'd been following. There was no way they'd be staying in the building now that it had been used to try to take him out.

Sure enough, as he crouched peering down onto the darkened streets like some sort of gargoyle sentinel, he caught a brief flash of colour a block over that was the same as the garish blue shirt Axel had been wearing. It was followed by the sound of a revving engine. In the time it took him to bound closer, they had already disappeared, leaving only the fading trace of their scent. Snarling in frustration, he slunk back to the meeting point he'd arranged with Angelo's people if they got separated.

At least he'd managed to press one of the tracking stickers behind Axel's ear when he'd greeted him in the gym by clasping him behind the neck like the wolves often did.

Marco's tech guy, Luca, should be able to follow the signal. That didn't sate his jaguar's need to tear into them for the injury he'd sustained that was still seeping blood and hurt like a bitch, though. It must've been a silver bullet from the burning sensation searing in his skin.

Rafe was going to kill him.

CHAPTER 10: RAFE

A familiar metallic scent filled the air as Adri stepped into the clinic, and Rafe's head snapped up as he let loose an involuntary rumbling growl that filled the room. He had his mate pinned to the wall in under a second, turning him gently to inspect the bullet hole that was still healing in his arm.

"What the fuck, kitten?"

"The bullet dropped out already. It'll be healed in no time."

"You're damn lucky it wasn't encapsulated silver nitrate."

"I'm fine, Doc."

"I need to examine you."

Adri rolled his eyes at him, and Rafe raised an eyebrow. "Are you winding me up on purpose? Is that how you want to play it?"

"Rafe? It sounds like you're busy!" Katie's cheerful voice called through the speaker from his laptop where they'd been looking at images of the melted device he'd found in the dead shifter's brain.

Pulling Adri along behind him because he couldn't stand

to let him go, Rafe moved back to the computer so he was in the video feed frame. "Thanks for your help, Katie. Let me know if you think of anything else."

"Of course. And if you get a live subject and need a consult, call me. Any time."

"You're not going to Rafe's clinic to perform surgery, babe!" Bella called in the background. She had a strict no contact with illegal business rule for her wife, although Katie was as independent as Adri was, so it didn't always work out how Bella hoped.

"I can give him pointers by video, sweetness," Katie replied over her shoulder. The idea of anyone calling the murderously scary woman '*sweetness*' was hilarious.

"Sorry to cut things short, but I need to go sort Adri out," Rafe said.

"Ah, yes! Your jaguar fighter! Is that him?"

Adri sent Rafe a quizzical look, but dutifully waved toward the camera. "Nice to meet you."

"I've been meaning to ask if we could borrow you for a fundraiser. One of the hospital board members got it into their head that we should run our own version of an amateur celebrity boxing tournament, and we can't seem to dissuade them from it. I want to sneak some professionals in there to reduce the likelihood that I spend the rest of the night dealing with avoidable concussions. You can still win the match, but your reflexes will mean you can avoid hurting them too badly while you do it."

"Katie's a neurosurgeon at the hospital," Rafe explained to Adri, who was looking even more confused.

"For humans?" Adri asked.

Katie laughed. "Yes. It's fun and rewarding. The best combo."

Bella had come into the shot now and was watching her wife indulgently. "Classic contrary cat shifter. Her folks forbid her from studying medicine, so of course she went and spent fifteen years at college to specialise in an area that was the least likely to be of use to her own kind."

Katie wrinkled her nose at her wife. "You love my contrariness. It's how I ended up with you."

Bella leaned down and gripped her throat, pulling her into a filthy kiss.

"And that's our cue to leave. Bye, ladies," Rafe said.

"Let me know the details, and I'll come help with your fundraiser," Adri added.

Ending the call, Rafe stood and turned to his mate, his eyes drawn back to the trail of red down his arm from his wound. His wolf was howling inside him at the thought that his mate had been hurt, that he could have lost him while he was sitting here chatting with his friend.

"Come upstairs and I'll clean you up," Rafe growled.

"I really am fine. Don't you dare waste your power healing me when my body can do it perfectly well on its own."

"And what if I want to use my power to do something else?"

Adri audibly swallowed, and Rafe pressed a firm hand to his muscled back, directing him up to the apartment.

"You shouldn't waste your power on that, either," Adri said.

Rafe's smile was all predatory teeth when Adri glanced back at him as they passed through the door to the bedroom. "Your pleasure is never a waste."

"If I let you have control here, it doesn't mean you get a say in where I go or what I do outside."

"I'm well aware," Rafe said, eyes drawn back to the dried blood on his mate's arm. "Now, come get clean. The blood and grime must be driving your jaguar crazy."

Rafe kept the lights dimmed and his movements slow as

he undressed them in the bathroom while the shower warmed. Stepping in behind Adri when it was ready, he grabbed a washcloth and soap, letting his power wash over his mate's skin along with the water to reassure himself that his mate was okay. That he was safe.

"Why does that feel so good?" Adri moaned as he leaned into Rafe's touch, sparking another surge of arousal through him.

"What are your limits, kitten?"

"Why? What do you want to do?"

Rafe sighed, softening his touch even further to teasing strokes. "If you want this, you need to communicate, sweetheart. But, sure, I'll start. My sole interest is your pleasure. If you're not into something, you tell me. Immediately. Be as rude as you like if it's about drawing a boundary in bed. Or just say stop. No biting to break skin unless you're prepared to bond. I can't control my wolf if you tease that way. I'm not into humiliation, yours or mine, beyond the thrill you'd get from being forced to orgasm wherever and whenever I choose like the good kitten I know you can be."

"Fuck," Adri groaned, his eyes squeezing shut as he squeezed the base of his cock like he was trying to stop himself from coming.

"Too much?" Rafe asked.

"No."

"Good. Now talk. You don't want anyone to have control over your life. What else?"

Rafe somehow managed to find the self-control to take his hands off his mate and start methodically washing himself as he waited for Adri to find his words.

"Holding me down is fine, but I really don't do well with restraints of any kind or being locked up, and I don't like being blindfolded. Whips and impact play are out, too. I get enough of that at work—impact, not whipping, obviously,"

Adri finally said, voice so quiet and rushed it almost blended in with the sound of the falling water splashing over them.

Rafe couldn't have stopped the growl his words sparked if he'd tried. He knew exactly why his kitten didn't like those things. Being trafficked for the fighting ring as a teen had left a lasting mark. Pulling Adri into his arms, Rafe nuzzled into his neck, dragging his scruff along the delicate skin so he could reestablish his scent on him.

"Did they hurt you any other way?"

"Not the way you're asking. Only being forced into the ring until I fought back."

Rafe wished he'd tortured the vampires who'd taken Adri longer. He'd tracked them down not long after they first met and made sure they'd never take another young person from their home. It didn't stop the flesh trade, of course. There were always more immoral assholes to take their place. But at least he knew his mate would never come face-to-face with the people who'd stolen his life from him on the street. Turning off the water, Rafe grabbed a warm towel to wrap around Adri's body.

"Everyone who touched you back then is gone," Rafe promised, as he got to his knees to pat his mate's feet and legs dry.

"I know. It pissed me off something chronic when I realised what you were doing."

"You wanted to kill them yourself?" Rafe asked.

Adri shrugged. "I couldn't back then. Not without getting in more trouble than I could get out of with Viviana. I hated that you could give that to me, and then you started pushing Viviana to move the gym and improve things for my fighters, and it just made me even more mad."

"Mad enough to avoid me for over a decade," Rafe said, getting back to his feet and pressing a kiss to Adri's jaw before heading to the bedroom.

"Only because I knew I'd lose myself to you the second I let you close."

"Oh, kitten. You're not going to lose anything. All I want is to give you everything you need to be truly free to be whoever you want. If you lost a part of yourself, it would be like losing a part of me, because you're the piece of my soul that walks the world outside my body."

Adri shuddered in his arms where they stood next to the bed. "I'm not ready for that," he whispered.

Rafe cupped his jaw, pressing a series of gentle kisses along his lush lips. "That's okay. I'll be right here waiting when you are, and we can still have all the fun with this chemistry between us in the meantime. You didn't mention any of the things I told you I could do with my power were a limit. Do you want to add anything to your list?"

Adri tilted his head up, his lips parting to let Rafe plunder his mouth. "No. Do your worst, Doc."

Rafe's soft smile turned predatory. "On the bed. Hands on the headboard."

Adri was all feline grace as he crawled onto the bed, arching his body in long, seductive lines as he stretched to follow Rafe's instructions.

"Fuck, you're beautiful," Rafe said, standing transfixed as he stared at the picture Adri made on his bed.

Starting at his ankle, Rafe set to work worshipping his mate, using tongue and teeth and fingers to draw a symphony of needy moans from Adri's mouth as he slowly worked his way up his body. His healing power thrummed beneath his skin, begging to be let loose, so he let a tiny trail seep into every spot he touched, knowing it would set Adri's blood aflame with arousal.

"Knees up, kitten," he ordered, when Adri's moans turned to muttered oaths.

"Rafe, please. Hurry up."

Rafe just raised an eyebrow and stared his mate down until he wrapped a hand around each leg to hold his knees apart, putting every inch of himself on display. Rafe groaned, reaching down to stroke his throbbing length that he'd been ignoring to try and give himself some relief.

"Prettiest thing I've ever seen," Rafe growled, watching Adri's cock kick in response to his voice as his balls sat high and heavy above his perfect, enticing hole.

Adri's entire body tensed and arched as Rafe dived in to lap at his rim with his long tongue. Sucking and gently nibbling, he'd barely got his first taste with the tip of his tongue when Adri's whole body tensed and his breathing became sharp and frantic. That wouldn't do.

"No. I'm not nearly done with you yet, kitten," Rafe chided, reaching up to roll his balls gently in his fingers and letting his magic soak into Adri's skin to stop him from coming until *Rafe* was ready.

"Fuck!" Adri cried as Rafe relaunched the assault on his hole, not bothering to hold back now he knew his mate couldn't orgasm and the pleasure would just build and build.

Pressing firmly with his tongue, he licked in deep, moaning as he felt the muscle contracting around him. Grabbing the lube off his side table, he managed to squirt some on his fingers, and probably all over the bed, before reaching up to slide his hand up and down his jaguar's impressive, ridged length as he continued his efforts to lick and suck his soul out of his body.

Adri's moans grew louder, his hands shifting from holding his knees apart to wrapping tight in Rafe's hair to hold him close as his legs splayed out across his sheets. His hips jerked up repeatedly in aborted thrusts as he tried to chase the pleasure Rafe's hand was giving him before pushing back onto his tongue.

"Rafe, please. I need to come," Adri begged.

"Are you sure about that, kitten?"

"Yes, dammit!"

"Okay, remember you asked for it, though."

Keeping up his firm strokes on Adri's cock, Rafe slid two fingers of his other hand in alongside his tongue, crooking them to find the perfect pressure that would send his mate soaring. Stroking with both his power and his hand, Rafe stopped holding back Adri's orgasm and instead forced him into an instant, overwhelming climax that had his screams echoing off the bedroom walls. He didn't stop working him over as the orgasm went on and on, nor did he let Adri's cock soften. When his cries became muffled sobs of need, Rafe paused only long enough to raise his head to meet his mate's eyes.

"You good?"

Adri just moaned, so he pulled back further.

"I need your words, kitten. Too much, or can I keep going?"

"More," Adri whimpered.

Grinning, Rafe lifted himself up so he could take Adri's cock into his mouth, letting his power soak in deep as he sucked him with purpose, quick and efficient, until Adri's eyes rolled back in his head and he cried out as Rafe pushed him into another orgasm.

"Oh my fucking god," Adri gasped.

Not giving him a moment to rest, Rafe crawled up his body, latching onto a nipple that had been lacking his attention and sucking it deep into his mouth, his tongue and teeth working it over as he used his still slick fingers to tug at the one on the other side.

"What the fuck? Nipple orgasms aren't a thing, are they?" Adri moaned, the instinctive thrusting of his hips dragging his still throbbingly hard cock along Rafe's stomach.

"Squeeze your legs together for me, kitten," Rafe gasped before shifting his mouth to his other nipple.

It was Rafe's turn to moan as Adri managed to create the perfect slick tunnel for his cock to thrust into between his thighs. The pleasure had him biting down on the nipple still sucked between his teeth and letting his power surge again to drag another orgasm from his mate. Adri's chest was thoroughly coated in cum now, his breathing sharp pants of overwhelmed need. The scent of Adri's pleasure saturated the space as Rafe dragged his body along his mate's, revelling in the dirty slide. He refused to come himself, though. Not until he was inside his mate.

"Fuck, Rafe. It hurts," Adri whimpered.

"Too much?"

"Hurts *good*. But I need…" Adri's voice trailed off as Rafe dragged his fingernails down his chest to start loosely stroking his gorgeous cock.

Fuck, his jaguar was perfect for him. "Take one more for me, kitten. Then I'll give you what you need."

CHAPTER 11: ADRI

"What the fuck? I can't … You can't … I've come three times already," Adri said, whimpering as his hips jerked up in a vain attempt to try to get Rafe to stroke his cock harder.

He'd never been so hard. Never ached so much. Never come so many times so quickly and had it only drive his arousal higher. Every part of his skin that touched his mate's vibrated with desire. His balls hurt like someone had been squeezing the cum right out of them, and somehow they were still full and desperate.

Rafe lifted his head from the exquisite torture he'd been wreaking on his nipples and brushed a soft kiss across his lips that had Adri chasing his mouth for more.

"Do you want me to stop?" Rafe asked, his face hovering over Adri's and his hand pausing where it had been working over his dick.

Adri huffed and squeezed his eyes shut. "No," he whispered.

"Good kitten," Rafe murmured, pressing another kiss to

his lips and tightening his grip to stroke him with more purpose.

Adri moaned into his mouth, shoving his tongue in to explore as Rafe finally let him jerk his hips up into his grip to take his pleasure from his hand.

"I need you inside me, dammit," Adri cried, frustration filling him as he tried to chase an orgasm he was too sexually exhausted to find.

"I can't risk taking that beautiful ass of yours tonight, kitten. I'd claim you as soon as I came. But give me one more and I'll slide up this bed and come between those lush lips of yours."

"Need it," Adri whined, too far gone to care about anything but *finally* making his mate come. "Help me."

"Always," Rafe said, right before another wave of that intoxicating moonlit magic thrummed through his cock and balls, ripping an orgasm from Adri that had his vision turning white.

His rhythmic screams of pleasure were cut off by the most delicious thing he'd ever tasted as Rafe pushed the thick head of his cock to his lips. He was so out of it he hadn't even noticed his mate moving. Adri tipped his face up, ripping his hands away from the headboard to dig his clawed fingers into Rafe's hips and position him so he could drive down into his throat the way he wanted.

Rafe groaned above him. "Tell me you want this," he said, somehow managing to pull his hips away so his cock wasn't resting on Adri's tongue anymore.

Adri tried to pull him back, but Rafe was too strong. Fuck, that was hot.

"I want it so bad I'm probably going to orgasm *again* just from feeling you come down my throat from fucking my face."

"You're so beautiful like this."

Adri pressed against Rafe's hips to pause him before he could slip his cock back between his lips, and the doc instantly stopped.

"What do you need, sweetheart?"

"I can take it as deep as you want, but I need to taste you when you come. Please."

Rafe's eyes flashed gold and his fangs lengthened, the racing of his heart a reassurance that Adri wasn't the only one completely overcome by this thing between them.

Done with talking now he'd said what he needed to say, Adri let his tongue slip out to lap at the head of Rafe's cock that was just in reach, knowing the rasping texture would drive him crazy.

"Going to spin around so I can watch you come untouched, just like you said."

"No magic this time. Save your strength," Adri said as Rafe repositioned them.

The angle was perfect now to take the wolf shifter right down his throat, so Adri didn't bother giving him any warning. He just tilted his head right back and dragged Rafe down to the root.

He hadn't been joking when he said he'd probably come again just from this. Somewhere between the third and fourth orgasms Rafe had coaxed from his body, he'd become hypersensitive, and all the wires in his body were well and truly crossed. It felt like it was harder to stop himself from coming than it was to come. How many times could he climax if Rafe didn't relent? He knew the answer. Only as many as he wanted. Only as many as he could safely have. Rafe wouldn't let anything else be true.

The feel of his mate's cock on his tongue was everything. Dizzy from arousal, desperate to please, he worshipped his length like he never had anyone before. Every sense was tuned in to Rafe's pleasure. He alternated sucking him deep and hard, with teasing licks and kisses that he could tell drove Rafe wild because he heard every caught breath, every skipped heartbeat. The scent of Rafe's arousal spiked each time he gave him pleasure, feeding his own.

The vibrations of Adri's moans of pleasure were what finally seemed to make Rafe lose control. His hips thrust down to bury his length in Adri's throat over and over again until tears were streaming down his cheeks and his saliva was slick down his chin in the best way. The gasping breaths Adri managed weren't quite enough to stop him becoming light-headed, and it only made the throbbing neediness in his groin even worse. His every sense was subsumed by Rafe. As he felt his mate's hips stutter and his cock thicken in his mouth, the pleasure grew overwhelming. It was Rafe pulling back to make sure he could taste the first spurt of his release that threw Adri over the edge one last time.

Adri's cries and moans had Rafe swearing as he pushed deep again to finish as far inside him as he could go while Adri's perfectly overstimulated cock jerked and shot all over his stomach, untouched. He was almost too blissed out drowning in his mate's pleasure to feel his own, but this release *finally* brought that bone-deep satisfaction he'd been seeking. The satisfaction of knowing he'd taken care of Rafe as well as he'd been taken care of.

When he finally managed to prise his eyes back open, it was to a warm cloth gently wiping down his oversensitive skin before Rafe pulled him into his arms. With his ear resting on Rafe's chest, he let himself sink into the moment to the soundtrack of his heartbeat.

"I can't believe you came again just from blowing me. You're perfection," Rafe murmured, bending to press a kiss to his forehead.

Adri groaned and hid his face in the soft hair of his chest. "Don't make it into a thing."

"Oh, it's definitely a thing," Rafe replied, voice still soft as he traced a hand up and down Adri's back, calming his still-trembling muscles. "How are you feeling?"

"Don't doctor me."

"I asked you a question, kitten," Rafe said, a hint of warning in his tone.

For once, Adri couldn't be bothered fighting him. "I'm fine."

Rafe tilted his chin up, forcing him to meet his gaze, his brow furrowed in concern. "If you're just fine after that, we did something wrong. *I* did something wrong."

Adri huffed in annoyance, wrapping his arm more tightly around Rafe where it rested at his waist. "More than fine, okay? I've never come so hard or so many times."

"Was it too much?"

"I can take whatever you've got, Doc."

"Yes, but do you want to? Did you let me do that for me or for you?"

Adri tried to look away, but Rafe wasn't having it. "Both."

Rafe's expression softened. "So good for me."

"There it is. Took it too far," Adri growled, sparking a laugh from Rafe. Fuck, he loved the sound of Rafe's laugh.

"Forced orgasms are okay, but praise after sex is a bridge too far?"

"Pretty much," Adri muttered, jerking his chin out of Rafe's grip so he could nuzzle into his neck instead.

They fell asleep like that—all wrapped up in each other—and when they woke the next morning to the buzz of a phone, somehow Adri had only twined himself even tighter around Rafe's body.

Adri grumbled as Rafe jostled his head reaching toward the bedside table. His claws slipped out of his fingers to knead Rafe's chest where his hand was resting palm down.

Rafe's soft hiss had Adri freezing and retracting them as he woke up enough to realise what he'd done.

"Sorry," he mumbled, nuzzling into Rafe's pec to lick the pinpricks he'd left and drawing in a deep breath of scent.

"Don't be sorry. I like it," Rafe said, placing a warm hand over his and twining their fingers together to keep it there as he checked his messages.

"Who's messaging at this hour?"

Rafe laughed and kissed his head. "It's ten in the morning already, sweetheart."

"Fuck. I need to tell Vee where I am. I'm usually there to help coach."

"Marco will have taken care of it already. Pretty sure she knows it's up to you when and how much you want to work now."

Adri stiffened and tried to pull away, but Rafe wouldn't let him go. "What the fuck did I say about not controlling my life, Doc?"

Rafe put the phone down and turned to face him, tilting his chin up and pressing a hard kiss to his lips that Adri did his best to resist, but found himself caving and opening up to regardless.

"You can keep doing exactly what you have been if you want. We made it so that you could control your life *more*. So no one can tell you where to be except you… and Marco when he needs you."

Adri rolled his eyes. "He's not my damn Alpha."

"So you don't want in on scoping out the location your friends from last night ended up at? It's a pack-only operation."

Adri scowled at him. Opened his mouth to tell him to fuck off. Thought better of it.

"Are you going?" he asked.

"Yes. Marco needs me to look over any medical equipment and wants me on hand in case we end up facing someone feral again."

Adri shivered. His memories of the fight were still a bit scattered, but he could remember looking into eyes with no humanity as his arm started to tear away from his body.

"Then I'm going, too. Someone needs to watch your back, and I might recognise any fighters there."

He really hoped he didn't, though. What if all the fighters he'd helped move on from the ring had just ended up in a warehouse somewhere being experimented on? His emotions must've been showing on his face, because Rafe pulled him close, wrapping him back in his arms.

"It'll be okay," Rafe murmured. "And if it isn't, we'll fix it together."

In all his years working for the Lunettis, Adri had only visited the pack lands a handful of times, and he'd never stepped much further into Marco's mansion than the front entryway and reception room. Rafe led him confidently through the front door, not bothering to knock, and directed him through to a study with a gentle hand at the small of his back.

The rest of the room was already full when they arrived. Marco was on a call behind his desk, his facial expressions giving nothing away. His cousin Emilio was perched on the edge of the desk, talking to his husband, Rocco. Silas, Marco's second, was deep in conversation with Luca, the hacker, over on one of the couches. A flash of movement caught his eye when they stepped inside as Bella waved a hand at him in greeting, keen interest in her eyes as she watched the way

Rafe's arm snaked around his waist as they headed to the only free seat.

"You take it," Adri said.

He might have met most of these people before, but they were still a dangerous bunch. He'd much rather be upright and able to move if he needed.

Rafe raised an eyebrow at him before dropping into the seat and pulling Adri along with him. He was so caught by surprise that he fell right into Rafe's lap, exactly where the irritating doc had meant for him to be. Twisting, he snapped his teeth at Rafe's throat as his strong arms wrapped around his waist, sparking a soft laugh from the doctor.

"I'd be thoroughly distracted if you were standing beside me with your fly right next to my face. This is much better," Rafe whispered in his ear.

The ridiculous statement somehow made him smile and shake his head instead of rage. He could feel the bulge of Rafe's cock against his ass where he sat on his lap, so he knew for sure this was going to be *way* more distracting. For both of them.

"Oh shit, did you finally lock down your jaguar, Doc?" Silas called from nearby, which of course had everyone turning to look at them.

Adri stiffened and opened his mouth to swear at the asshole, but Rafe snuck a hand under his shirt, stroking his skin. A gentle reminder that here, of all places, he needed to keep a civil tongue.

"If anyone locks him anywhere, I will make them die a very slow, very painful death," Rafe replied, voice dry.

"Alright, Doc. Message received," Silas said, smiling as he held his hands up in surrender. "Welcome to the family, Adrien."

Adri's scowl deepened, and Rafe pressed a kiss to his neck. "Play nice, Adri," he murmured.

"Sai, stop pulling the jaguar's tail just to see what he'll do," Marco said.

Silas smirked before turning to his Alpha, inclining his head. "What's the plan?"

Everyone quieted as all attention turned to Marco.

"For those who don't know already, last night Adrien followed two fighters suspected of being part of an unsanctioned fighting ring into vampire territory, where he was ambushed. He managed to get a tracker on one of the guys enroute before that, and we now have the address of where that tracker ended up. It's in an area with limited cameras to tap into, so all Luca's been able to track down is some grainy satellite footage and a collection of shell companies that own the location. He confirmed the links between the feral fighter and the unsanctioned ring. Rafe's research suggests the deaths were related to illegal medical research, most likely undertaken by the D-2S for unknown purposes."

"Well, fuck," Emilio said as Marco paused. "Does that mean we can go kill them now?"

"This is the best lead we've had on a physical location associated with the D-2S yet, but there's too much of a paper trail. It's sloppy compared to their usual MO. I doubt it's a significant site, but I'll take any lead I can get on whatever is turning these shifters feral. They won't stay there long if they're using it for something. We need to go in hard and fast tonight and get as much intel as we can. Rafe is coming to identify any medical equipment and run triage if things go wrong. Adri is there for any insight or knowledge of the fighters there. We'll confirm tactics once we've got eyes on the building. Any questions?" Marco continued.

"Given the history of explosives, Blaze is making a fire witch available to you, and I'll come along to keep your approach hidden," Rocco chimed in.

Marco tipped his head in thanks. "We'll roll out as soon as they're here, then."

"Will you shift when we get there?" Adri asked.

Rafe glanced over at him before looking back at the road as he drove the same SUV he'd used to get them to the fight.

"No. I need to carry medical supplies on me, and I prefer to have some clothes on if I'm patching people up in the middle of a gunfight."

Adri couldn't help but be a little disappointed. He'd never seen Rafe's wolf. It shouldn't matter. He hardly shifted himself because he'd spent so long ignoring and suppressing that side of himself as a child, only to have it exploited as an adult. Watching the way the Lunetti Pack had been together had reinforced what he might be missing out on by keeping himself aloof, though. Maybe a pack wasn't all bad.

A strong hand reached out to squeeze his thigh. "You want to see my wolf, kitten? I'll show you whenever you want. Or you can come run with me in the forest one night with the pack."

Adri shrugged, not ready to admit what he wanted yet. "I'm going to shift."

His senses were much more acute in jaguar form. He'd be better able to make sure no one snuck up on his doc while he was busy. Plus, he wasn't interested in wielding a gun, and his bite force when shifted was an excellent weapon.

"I'll do my best not to let your beautiful jaguar distract me, then."

Adri rolled his eyes. Rafe was ridiculous sometimes.

"I'm serious, kitten. I can barely tear my eyes off you in either form. If you're going to use your cat senses, could you see if you can sniff out anything that might be a neural chip? It's probably too much to hope there's one with brain matter on it that will make it easy to scent, but you should be able to pick up on the scent of solder if it's somewhere it shouldn't be."

"Yeah, Doc. I can do that, but I'm sticking close to you."

"Good—" Rafe swallowed back the '*kitten*' at the end of that sentence, clearly thinking better of it, and Adri couldn't decide if that made him more or less annoyed.

"Are we heading back into vampire territory again?" Adri asked, peering at the surrounding streets as they crossed one of the three boundary roads that trisected the city.

"Yeah, Marco's been talking to Darius about it. If we find evidence that Kyan is involved with the D-2S, he's going to have to move up his plans to take over the coven, whether he's ready or not. We can't leave that kind of threat in charge of a third of the city, and we can't trust the Council to deal with it without going full nuclear option and replacing all of us."

Adri's brow furrowed as he considered this information. He'd been peripherally aware of the power plays in the city, of course. You couldn't avoid it when you worked for the Lunettis. But no one had ever trusted him with any sort of detail about it.

"I thought the Council was there to maintain order."

Rafe scoffed under his breath. "They're there to maintain power. *Theirs*. But to do that, they need to be perceived as the least bad option by the vast array of supernatural communities they deal with. Some individuals who work for them are fine. They have morals. They genuinely want to keep people safe. Rocco's family is like that. Marco had to quietly look into them before we finalised the marriage arrangement with the MC. The rest range somewhere from unknown to dangerous power-trip."

"Should you be telling me things about Rocco and the Council? Isn't he part of the Lunetti family now?"

"So are you, kitten, and you can't be part of Marco's inner circle without understanding the political context we're operating in."

Adri's head whipped round to glare at Rafe. "I'm not part of that, though!"

"You don't get to decide who we let close. If I have my way, you'll be on my lap at every meeting I attend from here on out."

Adri swallowed hard. How had things between them changed so quickly? "What if I betray you?"

"You would never hurt me, kitten. Not like that. But you can keep kneading me with those delightful claws as much as you like."

Adri looked down in surprise to find his hand had migrated to Rafe's leg without him realising, and he was, in fact, digging his partially shifted fingers into the fabric and scratching at his skin. A hot flush spread up his neck to his face.

"Sorry—"

Rafe grabbed his hand and kept it pinned where it was before he could pull away. "Never apologise for being your truest self, Adri. I love watching you settle into who you were always meant to be. Just like I love feeling your claws claiming my skin."

"That's not what I'm doing," Adri huffed, ignoring his jaguar's protest in the back of his mind that it was exactly what they were doing and how much better his scent stuck to their mate when he implanted it with his claws.

"We're almost to our staging point," Rafe said, gesturing to a darkened warehouse ahead that Adri recognised as one of the venues for their fights.

The fighting ring that operated throughout the city

provided excellent cover for Marco to acquire property in other territories, he realised. Then he shook his head and told himself to focus. He didn't need to be trying to familiarise himself with Marco's methods and strategies. No matter what Rafe said about him becoming part of his inner circle.

Rafe pulled the SUV right through the large doors and into the darkened building. Adri blinked in surprise as they crossed the threshold and light flooded over them to reveal half a dozen other vehicles parked neatly in the space and a group of predatory-focussed shifters standing around a table in the centre.

"What the fuck?" Where had they all come from?

Rafe parked the vehicle and reached over to undo Adri's seatbelt for him while he stared around in surprise before kissing the scruff on his jaw. "Rocco is an expert in glamour and illusion. You wouldn't have noticed after your fight with the feral fighter, but Rocco used his magic to keep the whole place and all the crowd fleeing from drawing police attention. He's one of the most powerful air witches in the country. We're lucky to have him."

He'd known being involved with Rafe and his pack was going to be next level, but this really hit it home. What was he thinking, trying to fit in with these people?

"We wouldn't even know where to look without your help, Adri. You belong here as much as anyone. You belong with me," Rafe murmured, somehow picking up on the thoughts he hadn't expressed.

For a split second, Adri considered leaving. Then he realised that would mean relying on someone else to watch Rafe's back. That wasn't something he was willing to do.

"Whatever. Let's do this already," he said, stepping out of the car.

Adri hung back as the pack discussed how they'd go

about breaching the location of the tracker, not willing to draw any more attention to himself.

"The building is a decommissioned office block. Four levels and a basement carpark," Marco said.

"Our scan shows one guard on the main entrance, one on the carpark elevator, and half a dozen people concentrated on the second floor," Rocco added.

"The limited number of people suggests either this isn't a significant location, or they've already mostly cleared out," Marco continued. "None of our magical or technical scans suggest the building itself has been wired with explosives, but given the D-2S history, we have to assume the occupants might be. There's also a chance the people here are just fighters associated with the ring and don't know anything about the group. Given the variables, I want to send Rafe in first, undercover as a doctor visiting, and see if we can avoid triggering an incendiary response that would destroy any intel."

"No!" Adri growled before he could stop himself.

They could send his mate alone into a building filled with terrorists over his dead body.

CHAPTER 12: RAFE

Marco's eyes flashed gold as he glared at Adri over the table, and it was all Rafe could do not to step between them.

"Watch your tongue, Carter. I'm not going to send him alone. You're going with him," Marco said.

Rafe suppressed a growl. He didn't know which was worse—leaving Adri behind to deal with the pack without him and risk him pissing off his Alpha, or bringing him into the middle of a potential terrorist cell that had already ambushed him once.

"They'll recognise the two of them as associated with the pack," Luca pointed out, glancing up from his computer. "I can't hack anything to stop them recognising their faces."

"I *want* them to know they're pack. Rafe will tell them we're more concerned about the recent deaths than the existence of the fighting ring, and that the cost of their continued operation is submitting to a medical check by us. If they're not associated with the D-2S, the fact that it's the doc visiting and not an enforcer should head off any violence and give you a chance to scope things out. He's the closest thing we have to a peaceful envoy. If things go south, the rest of us will be right here as backup. Rocco can keep us hidden under a glamour near the entrance. Rafe and Adri are more than capable of holding their own long enough for us to get there."

Unless someone exploded. Or opened fire with silver nitrate bullets. Or they all turned feral. There were so many ways this could go wrong, but Marco's plan was the best option they had, given the history of how quickly any sources of information died when the D-2S realised they were under threat.

"They already ambushed Adri once. Why risk sending him in at all?" Rafe said, sparking a huff of frustration from his mate.

"There's a big difference between luring a solo fighter into an ambush and attacking someone who walks up to the door representing the Lunettis. They're not going to risk pissing me off. And if I keep him here, he's going to charge in to rescue you the second something feels off. I can't afford to be distracted containing a pissed-off jaguar," Marco said.

"Fucking hell. I can control myself," Adri snapped.

"Not when those instincts you're so set on ignoring are riding you hard. You're best-placed to recognise the fighters and what's going on with them in there. Would you really rather stay behind?" Marco asked, raising an eyebrow.

"No. I'm not leaving the doc unprotected. Can we get on with this already?" Adri said, his sullen voice belied by his keen predatory focus as he shifted his weight to the balls of his feet like he was prepping for a fight.

Warmth filled Rafe's chest despite the tense circumstances as his wolf basked in the satisfaction of his mate's protectiveness.

The guard at the entrance drew her weapon on them the second Rafe and Adri stepped past the edge of Rocco's glamour to approach the abandoned office building. Every instinct screamed at him to place himself between his mate and the danger, but he had to trust in his packmates hidden behind them to keep them safe. Rocco wouldn't let a bullet reach them out here, but once they were inside, it would be a different matter.

Adri was carrying the bag of medical equipment that was their cover, his nonchalant swagger portraying false indifference to the threat. Raising his hands to show he wasn't armed, Rafe kept his slow pace walking forward, letting the dominance of his wolf loose to roll over the shifter taking aim at them.

"Put that away unless you want to make an enemy of Alpha Lunetti. We're here to help, not harm. This time," Rafe called.

"Stop where you are!" the woman called back. She smelled of wolf and fear.

Rafe let his hands drop to his side and kept walking. "You're a wolf in vampire territory without the protection of a pack. Are you really going to make it worse by attacking me? I'm here to help. I'm a doctor."

"*He's* not," the woman said, jerking her chin at Adri.

Something wasn't right here. He knew the Lunetti Pack was intimidating, but no one put a terrified guard on the entrance to their building if they could help it.

"He's my mate," Rafe said, sparking a grumble of annoyance from Adri.

"Are we just announcing that to everyone now?" he hissed.

Rafe's lips twitched as he suppressed a grin, but he didn't take his eyes off the woman. "Two of your fighters have been brutally, publicly murdered in the last week."

The woman shrugged, the gun still trained on him. "I don't know anything about that."

"Our Alpha needs the incidents to stop. I'm not here to cause trouble or shut you down. I'm just here to examine you all and make sure no one else dies."

"Wait here," the woman said, her hands shaking as she finally holstered her weapon and stepped through the glass door of the old office block to call someone on a radio.

She must've really been stressed, because she didn't even seem to realise she was talking loud enough that he could still hear. He could only make out her side of the conversation, but he could tell whoever she was speaking with was pissed off. Her eyes searched the road behind them as she talked, Rocco's magic doing its job to keep their backup hidden as she reassured whoever she'd called that they'd come alone.

"Okay, you can come in," she said at last. "But you can't roam the facility. I'll bring the fighters down here to meet you."

That was fine. He'd figure out how to scope the location once he'd started his examinations.

"I'll start with you," Rafe said, rescuing his bag from Adri and setting it down on the dusty reception desk nearby.

"I don't fight in the ring," the woman said, pretending nonchalance as she messaged someone, presumably the fighters.

Rafe didn't miss the way her eyes had widened in surprise at his offer, though. Or the way she stared at him like he might hold the answer to a question she was too terrified to ask. As he tried to puzzle out what was going on with her, Adri stepped closer to murmur in his ear.

"There are at least two video cameras monitoring us. Someone's listening."

That explained the mismatch he was seeing between her words and her body language.

"What's your name?" Rafe asked, his voice softening despite himself. He'd always had a weak spot for those in trouble.

"Doesn't matter."

"Come stand in front of me," Rafe said, reaching into his bag to take out an old-school stethoscope.

The tool was just a prop, an excuse to stand close to her and touch her without clueing in the people watching through the cameras that he was using his magic to scan her body. The true extent of his healing ability was something he and Marco were careful to keep under wraps.

"Can't you hear my heartbeat without that thing?" the woman asked, stepping in front of him just like he'd asked.

"Yes, but with extra amplification, I can pinpoint any issues exactly. May I?"

The woman nodded.

She was wearing a dark purple top with a scoop neck that gave him the access he needed. Pressing the diaphragm of the scope over her heart, he let his magic wash through that point as subtly as he could. Hopefully, she'd attribute any weird sensation to the cold temperature of the metal against her hot skin.

The sense of wrongness coming from her struck so hard it was all he could do not to rock back. Letting his power flow up to her brain, he sensed a foreign object embedded there. One that was interfering with the function of her energy, with the essence of the wild magic that flowed through her veins and made her the shifter she was.

His eyes had dropped to the point where the stethoscope rested on her chest as he focussed his attention beneath her skin. As he looked up to meet her gaze, he saw the knowledge of the violation the terrorists had forced on her in her eyes.

"Help me," she mouthed, her head carefully angled away from the cameras.

Before he could reply, the glass wall looking out to the street shattered inward, firing shards of glass like shrapnel around them. Snarling as his bare arms were sliced to shreds, Rafe spun to face the new threat, barely processing the flash of purple that was the guard sprinting deeper into the building, away from the attackers.

Adri had already shifted. The tang of his mate's blood on the air enraged Rafe's wolf as he watched the jaguar prowl toward the street, his black fur all too visible in the harsh lighting of the office building. He was a walking target.

The sound of his packmates' growls only registered for a split-second before all his attention was focussed on three silent, impossibly fast figures closing in on his mate. Where the fuck had the vampires come from? He didn't have time to stop and find out. Shifting into his wolf form to give himself some protection from their mind tricks, he lunged to bite hard into the back of the knee of the nearest vampire targeting Adri. The metallic taste of blood filled his mouth as he hamstrung the attacker, immediately following up his advantage by lunging up the vampire's tumbling body to rip his throat out.

If these were Kyan's people, he couldn't risk permanently dispatching them, so he was careful to avoid severing the guy's spine with his teeth. The arterial spray across the granite flooring and the hunk of trachea he spat on the ground told him this one wouldn't be getting up anytime soon, though. Even with vampire healing.

A yowl to his right had him spinning back toward Adri, who was pinned down by two more of their attackers. Howling in anger, Rafe let his healing magic flow out before him in a rush of power that had the vampire's muscles seizing. It wouldn't last long before the magic inherent in their essence would fight off his attack. He took full advantage by bowling them out of the way to clear a path to his mate.

Adri had held his own as much as a single young shifter could against two older vampires. Large gashes from his claws had rent the face of one of them, and the other was sporting a broken wrist. Dropping his head, Rafe nudged Adri further away from the vampires, nipping at his haunches until his mate got the message to move outside, closer to their pack.

"Keep touching him and your death will be more painful than you can possibly imagine," a voice was growling—Emilio's.

As they emerged from the building, Rafe took in the scene on the street. Eight more vampires spread across the front of the building—half poised to rush into the building, and half facing off against Marco and the rest of the pack. Rocco's glamour hadn't held. They were no longer hidden. The reason for that became clear as Rafe turned his nose towards Rocco's crisp winter scent to see that he'd been pinned to the nearest wall by Kyan's hand at his throat.

Sending his power out in a quick scan, Rafe breathed a sigh of relief as he realised Rocco wasn't physically harmed. Yet. He was, however, being held in thrall by whatever Kyan's vampire powers were, unable to use his air magic. The head of the vampire coven must have snuck up on him while everyone was distracted, or Rocco would have used his power to protect himself before it could come to this.

Shifting so he could reassure Emilio, Rafe made his way to where Marco was holding back from launching himself at Kyan.

"He's not hurt," Rafe said softly.

"I *know* that. I can feel it myself. Let me go so I can rip the tendons out of Kyan's arms and use them to hang him," Emmy growled.

Everywhere he looked, eyes were flashing gold and silver with aggressive wild magic shining through.

"Let him go before you start a war, Kyan," Marco called.

"You're in *my* territory, wolf. You don't give the orders. If you didn't want to start a war, you shouldn't have come," Kyan drawled back.

Adri slipped closer, pressing his furred side to the front of Rafe's legs and screening his naked body from view as he placed himself between Rafe and the coven leader. The stubborn jaguar ignored his efforts to nudge him to the side and out of the line of fire. Not that there was anywhere safe now. The scents of more vampires approaching carried on the cold breeze, warning him they were now surrounded.

Before Marco could respond to Kyan's challenge, searing hot flames flared up around them, shielding their backs from the gathering vampire coven. He'd forgotten Rocco had brought a fire witch as backup to deal with any explosives. It wasn't going to help, though. Kyan had them at his mercy so long as his taloned hand was wrapped around Rocco's throat, and he knew it. All it would take was a sharp twist, and he'd snap the air witch's neck. That might be survivable from the magical benefits Rocco acquired when he bonded with Emmy, so Kyan would likely follow up by ripping his head from his body. There wouldn't be any coming back from that.

"We're only here to check out a potential terrorist cell and ensure there are no further incidents with the fighters that would bring the Council down on both our heads. You heard Gray at the winter ball. If we can't work together to stop the D-2S attacks from being noticed by the humans, they'll get rid of all our families and replace us here," Marco said, his voice carefully neutral despite the murderous glint in his eyes and his lengthened fangs.

"Uh, about that," the fire witch called from nearby, something in his voice drawing everyone's attention.

Rafe winced as he let his gaze flick in his direction. Standing next to the witch's side was the very thing they'd been trying to avoid—a seething mad vampire dressed in Council garb, her eyes flashing bright silver as her voice cracked out like a whip across the supernaturals gathered on the darkened street.

"What the *fuck* is going on here? You've got five seconds to stand down and explain yourselves before I call this in."

"There's no need for that, Leah. This was a simple disagreement," Kyan said, releasing his hold on Rocco and holding his hands out to his sides as he moved closer to the Council vampire.

The move didn't fool anyone into thinking he wasn't a threat, but at least with Rocco free of his grasp, they had options.

"The flames were visible from five blocks away."

The now-familiar thrum of Rocco's magic tingled against Rafe's senses before the air witch spoke up.

"They're hidden now. Nothing to see here."

Leah rolled her eyes. "Yeah, that's not going to work for me. Give me one good reason not to call Gray in."

Rafe cocked his head as he watched the Council rep with interest. It wasn't like them to hold back or give second chances. Why was she hesitating?

"We're doing exactly what Gray asked of us—hunting down the people responsible for the attacks in the city," Marco said.

The Alpha positioned himself between Rafe and the threat from Kyan and the Council rep, the rest of the pack gathering close behind them. Fangs and eyes flashed in the darkness as everyone failed to hide their aggression.

Adri shifted back to his human form as the tension grew, leaning close to whisper in Rafe's ear.

"She's been fucking Vee in secret."

His mate's words were too quiet for anyone further than a foot away to hear, but Marco's eyes flicked to Adri and away, his mouth twitching into a hint of a smirk. Rafe tugged Adri closer, nuzzling into his neck as his fangs ached to mark him up and reward him for the information he'd shared. Viviana would've told Marco herself if she thought the information was needed, but the fact Adri hadn't even hesitated before prioritising helping the pack over his relationship with Viviana was telling.

"Rocco, can you keep my conversation with Leah private?" Marco asked, loud enough for everyone to hear.

Kyan's glare in response was sharp and promised murder.

"Sure thing, Alpha," Rocco murmured.

"No one needs to be having any private conversations," Leah snapped.

"Are you sure about that?" Marco asked, raising an eyebrow.

Kyan moved closer in a blur of movement, sharp fangs shining in the night as he leaned in to speak to Marco.

"I don't know what you've got on her, but if I'm kept from that conversation, there will be consequences."

Rocco's magic flowed around them, and Rafe tipped his nose up to the air, scenting the change. He could still hear his Alpha's conversation just fine, but Leah's face on the other side of the road had settled into a scowl.

Movement from the building nearby caught Rafe's eye. His brow furrowed as he realised the people they'd come to investigate were taking advantage of the distraction to get out of there.

Leaning in close to Adri, Rafe whispered into his ear. "Can you go see what you can find before they destroy any evidence?"

Adri turned to him with a snarl. "I'm not leaving you here unprotected," he hissed.

"I'll watch your mate. No one will notice if you slink off. Any of the rest of us would draw attention," Silas whispered. Marco's second must have had the same thought as Rafe and moved closer.

"We don't have time to argue, Adri. Please?" Rafe murmured.

"If you die while I'm in there, I'll kill you," Adri snapped, his form blurring as he shifted back to his jaguar form.

"Back at you, kitten," Rafe whispered, his protective instincts warring inside him. He didn't want to let his mate out of his sight, but he also didn't want him to stay on the street where he would no doubt throw himself in front of the next vampire to try and attack Rafe.

Adri's tail lashed in annoyance against his thigh as he slipped unnoticed between the pack members who'd gathered close and back toward the building they'd just left. His movements were hidden by a combination of his feline stealth and Rocco's power.

A large hand blocked Rafe's view as he strained to keep watching his mate, and he glared at Silas as he dragged on the sweats he'd brought for him.

"He'll be fine. Better in there than here if we can't get this under control," Silas murmured, his eyes locked back on where Kyan was facing off against the Council rep.

"Enough with the privacy spells. Do I need to call in reinforcements?" Leah called, her growing frustration clear.

Marco waved a dismissive hand in her direction and didn't take his eyes off Kyan, who'd stalked closer to the Alpha while they were distracted. Rafe and the rest of the pack kept watch over the rest of the vampires nearby as the two men spoke.

"You breached the founding agreement when you came here without my permission," Kyan said, turning his back on the Council rep in dismissal as he faced down Marco, his words hidden from her listening ears by Rocco's spell.

"You breached it first by letting terrorists operate out of your territory. If we don't present a united front, this place will be swarming with Council operatives. Do you really think they won't find something to link you to what's happening?"

"I had no involvement in this. I don't work with *humans,*" Kyan sneered.

"You use whoever you can to get what you want, and right now, we both want the Council to get their noses out of our business. So pretend you're using me to do it if it makes you feel better and *get the fuck out of my way.*"

"Fine. Be a good puppy and go get the little vampire working for the enemy under control for me," Kyan said, stepping to the side and sweeping his arm out toward Leah.

Every pack member surrounding them snarled in response to the insult to their Alpha, but Marco just rolled his eyes at Kyan, shoulder-checking him on the way past.

Rocco's sound-dampening spell narrowed to keep whatever conversation Marco was having with Leah from everyone but the two of them. Rafe kept his eyes trained on the coven leader and the vampires who'd encircled their position while they waited, every sense alert for the violence poised on a hair-trigger to restart. His instincts were screaming at him to turn back to the building and seek out his mate, but that would only draw attention to Adri's absence.

Long minutes passed as Marco and Leah silently argued. They were still at it when Rafe felt a familiar presence at his back, Adri's jaguar butting his head against the side of his leg before his mate shifted back and accepted a spare pair of sweats from Rafe.

"Find anything?" Rafe asked softly, all too aware that the

vampires had moved closer and would hear everything now that Rocco's power was focussed elsewhere.

"Whoever was there from the fighting ring is either dead or cleared out of the building."

Rafe glanced over his shoulder at the broken glass and shadows as Adri quickly dressed. Fuck. Another dead end. All they had to show for their efforts was what he'd managed to sense with his power in the guard's brain.

"Or maybe there was nothing there to start with. Your Alpha will answer for this incursion," Kyan said.

Adri's growl rumbled in the air at the threat emanating from the vampire, and Rafe reached out to grip his nape before his impulsive mate tried to take on a fight he had no hope of winning. Kyan was far too old and powerful for the young shifter to face.

"The scouts you had destroying evidence are tied up in the basement when you're ready to collect them," Adri snapped back. "I wonder what the Council would think of the fact that they slit the throats of everyone we needed to question."

"I'm sure it was self-defence."

"It was a fucking execution I watched with my own eyes," Adri growled.

Silas jumped in before Rafe could, doing his bit to avoid outright war while their Alpha was occupied. "Neither of our families followed protocol. Let's call this one even and leave it at that."

Leah's voice calling broke the stand-off as Kyan glared daggers at Marco's second. "Sounds like you've worked out your differences. Alpha Lunetti has convinced me that the exposure risks here were managed. If you all go the fuck home without starting any more trouble, I don't see any reason to report this."

Kyan spun, abandoning his argument with Silas to stalk

closer to Leah as the blood magic he was gathering to himself made Rafe's senses roil. "What does Marco have on you, traitor?"

Leah held her ground. "You agreed to uphold the Accord, and by extension, the Council, the same as everyone else. My job there doesn't make me a traitor."

"But whatever arrangement you have with the wolf pack does."

"I was never going to remain in the Coven regardless of where I ended up, Kyan."

There was a story there. Rafe wondered if Viviana might know what it was, given how cosy Adri said she'd been with the Council vampire.

"Exactly. Traitor."

Leah rolled her eyes and turned her back on the coven leader, stalking away. It was a bold move. A reckless one. She clearly had history with Kyan that the rest of them were unaware of. Marco shifted a step to the left, placing himself between Kyan and the Council vampire, and Silas moved to join him.

"Neither of us wants her to change her mind. We've wasted enough time here tonight. Let's not waste more," Marco said.

Rafe held his breath as he waited to see which way Kyan was going to fall. The coven leader hadn't consolidated enough power yet to risk an attack from his brother if he decided to make a play for power, but he was close. Especially if he had an arrangement going with the D-2S in any capacity. The threat of Council retribution must've been enough to sway him, though, because the gathered coven enforcers melted into the shadows a moment later without any visible sign from Kyan—creepy vampire mind tricks.

"Agreed. Now get the fuck out of my territory," Kyan growled, buttoning up his tailored suit jacket like he'd just finished a business meeting and it wasn't coated in blood from the earlier ambush before leaving in a blur of motion so fast it was like he'd disappeared.

"Asshole," Adri murmured, sparking laughs from their nearby pack mates.

"Takes one to know one," Silas teased.

Adri flipped him his middle finger, and Rafe smiled as he wrapped an arm around his mate and directed him back toward the SUV. Marco caught his eye and gave him a nod as they left. They might not have found the information they were looking for, but the way Adri had stepped up for the pack and bonded with them more than made the night's risk worthwhile.

CHAPTER 13: ADRI

The second the doors of the car shut behind them, Rafe was all up in Adri's space, dragging his sexy salt-and-pepper beard over his neck to scent-mark him. With his jaguar still riding his instincts hard and the adrenaline of the attack still racing through his system, Adri found himself tilting his head to give the doc better access, sparking a low, rumbling sound of approval from Rafe.

"I'm *not* submitting. Cats don't do that," Adri complained, moaning as Rafe nuzzled into his skin and caught his skin between sharp teeth.

Before they could get too distracted, Adri pulled away and tapped Rafe's pocket. "Did you find my little present for you?"

Rafe's brow raised in question, and Adri reached into his sweats, pulling out the neural chip he'd found when he was scouting the building and carefully carried back in his jaguar's mouth.

"When did you put this there?" Rafe asked, inspecting the chip.

"Before I shifted back, when I head-butted you. I didn't want Kyan to see. I hope I didn't damage it with my teeth."

"It's intact. You did good, kitten. Really good."

Rafe's phone buzzed with an incoming message before Adri could respond to the praise with either violence or affection. The warmth his words had sparked was an uncomfortable sensation he chose to ignore.

As close as they were sitting, Adri could read the text over his shoulder, his jaguar purring inside him as his eyes traced over Rafe's strong, veined hands as he held the phone.

Alpha: I know you want to get your kitten back to your apartment but I need you both back home to regroup.

Adri huffed under his breath. "The pack lands aren't *my* home."

Rafe didn't glance up as he typed out a quick reply. "You're my mate. *I'm* your home, and the pack lands are my wolf's territory. That makes it your home."

"Rafe," Adri whined, exasperated by the way his doc refused to let him pretend this thing between them was anything other than what it was.

Rafe tipped his chin up, pressing a soft kiss to his lips that had Adri's eyes slipping half-closed. "Don't think too hard about it, kitten."

Adri huffed again and used the excuse of putting his seatbelt on to break the too-deep moment between them. Rafe didn't push again as they drove toward the Lunetti Pack lands. He just reached out and placed one of his big hands on Adri's thigh as he drove, squeezing gently. Adri stared out the window at the streetscape blurring by and pretended he hadn't noticed. From the corner of his eye, he could see Rafe's mouth stretched in a soft smile as he manoeuvred them through the city one-handed. Why was that so hot?

The SUV's headlights were the only illumination as they drove down the long driveway toward the pack house in the depths of the night. The crunch of tyres on gravel, the thrum of the engine, and the soft sounds of owls in the distance the only noises breaking the silence.

Adri's jaguar pouted inside him when Rafe finally took his hand off his leg as he slid the SUV into one of the underground car parks. Rolling his eyes at his own ridiculousness, Adri unlatched his seatbelt, only to have the door opened for him before he could reach the handle. It was hard to be annoyed when his usually serious doc flashed him a wicked grin as he stood there waiting for Adri to exit, knowing full well that Adri didn't want to be coddled that way.

"You're insufferable," Adri said, resisting the urge to press himself to Rafe's body as he got out.

"You seemed to enjoy my brand of suffering just fine when we were in bed," Rafe shot back.

The internal access up into Marco's private house that he shared with his closest family led them through a back corridor filled with a scent that had Adri's mouth watering. He'd never been in this part of the mansion before, and Rafe directed him toward the smell until they found the rest of Marco's family who'd been out with them gathered around a large island in the kitchen. Teasing and laughter shot back and forth as they served themselves from a selection of baked pies so fresh that someone must've been busy baking while they were facing down the coven.

Adri let himself be manoeuvred onto one of the barstools and sat watching in careful silence as Rafe fetched them a slice of something that smelled of cherries and apples.

"How did you know that's my favourite?" Adri asked, keeping his voice soft.

"I know everything about you, kitten."

"Aww… am I going to have to give up the title of chief stalker?" Rocco asked from nearby. The air witch looked pale, with dark circles like bruises beneath his eyes. He'd expended a great deal of power for the pack.

"Sit down before you fall down," Rafe said, eyes scanning him in concern as he left Adri's side to manhandle Rocco onto a cushioned window seat where he could recline if he needed to.

"Hey! How would you feel if I touched Adri like that?" Emilio complained.

"Just fine if you were making sure he didn't hurt himself," Rafe shot back.

"Shall we test that theory out?" Silas asked, stepping closer to Adri and sparking a full-on growl from Rafe that had everyone cracking up.

Adri felt heat rise in his cheeks, but kept his thoughts to himself. The last thing he wanted to do was encourage the Lunettis to double down on their teasing.

"Where's Marco?" Rafe asked Silas, returning to Adri's side and scooping up a bite of pie from his untouched plate before holding it up to Adri's mouth.

"I can feed myself," Adri muttered.

"Indulge me," Rafe whispered in his ear, sparking a full-body shiver in response.

Flashing him a glare, Adri reluctantly opened his mouth and let the doc feed him.

"He's sorting out the agreement he made with Leah to keep the Council off our backs. He'll be back shortly," Silas said.

That was interesting. What had Marco offered the vampire to withhold information from her employer like that? When Marco emerged with both Leah and Viviana in tow twenty minutes later, Adri had a suspicion what it might be. And that, in combination with the specific request that Adri join them at this meeting, gave him a sinking feeling in his gut. Sensing the sudden tension in him, Rafe leaned in close to rest his chin on Adri's shoulder and wrap his arms around him from behind.

"Just hear him out," Rafe whispered, so quiet even the nearby shifters wouldn't have been able to catch his words.

Silence fell as everyone turned their attention to their Alpha and the two women. Viviana had her arm draped around Leah's shoulders. The vampire was leaning into her side, her expression wary as she took in how many shifters were looking her way. Adri had seen Viviana's hook-ups come and go over the years, and he immediately knew this was something else from the level of intensity between them.

Was that what people saw when they looked at him and Rafe? Fuck.

"Kyan's already tried to retaliate against Leah for shutting them down tonight," Marco said. "He's not going to let this slide regardless of her position with the Council, and Leah can't go to her boss without admitting the conflict of interest from her relationship with Viviana. I've offered the pack's protection, but they can't stay in the city. Viviana's going to take her to her family out of state."

"Kyan will follow them," Vin pointed out from where he was nestled in close to Angelo. What was with all these mated pairs?

"Already taken care of. I won't let him touch her. We're going to fake Leah's death and disappear off the grid. He'll suspect something's up, but he's never seen us together. He shouldn't come looking for her at my family's ranch, and if he sends anyone after us, they won't live long," Viviana said, her determined gaze meeting Adri's as she spoke.

"What about the gym? Our people?" he asked.

"I need you to look after them for me."

Adri's vision narrowed as he fought to control his breathing. The last thing he wanted was to leave the fighters he protected with his life to some stranger to manage, but taking on responsibility for the fighting ring was a level of responsibility he didn't even want to contemplate the implications of. Marco didn't let him hide from it, though.

"If you do this, you need to admit that you're pack. I can't have someone managing my interests who can't acknowledge he owes allegiance to me," Marco said.

Adri glared at him. "You know I don't see it that way."

Marco held his gaze, his dominance cloying the air between them as Alpha power glittered in his eyes. "This is the only way I'll put you in the position. If you can't handle that, someone else will have control of their lives, and deep down, you'll still know that I'm your Alpha."

Adri's fangs lengthened and his fingertips tingled as his claws threatened to break free. Only Rafe's solid presence at his back kept him from doing something the Alpha would take as a threat.

"That's coercion," he growled.

"That's pack," Marco corrected. "I'm responsible for keeping my people safe. Part of that is making sure my leadership is seen as untouchable, and the pack's loyalty unquestioned. Otherwise, we'll end up with another traitor—or worse."

"Easy, kitten. Take a breath. He's not saying anything you didn't already know," Rafe murmured.

Adri tried to tug out of Rafe's arms, but the movement was half-hearted at best, and the doc just held him tighter. Annoyingly, the extra pressure and his mate's scent reduced the panicked sense of being backed into a corner that had his jaguar lashing out inside him.

"There's no one else I'd trust with them, Carter. Suck it up," Viviana said, her voice firm and her words reminding him of a hundred other times he'd heard that refrain from her mouth as she helped train the fighters over the years.

Fuck. It's not like he hadn't always known he worked for

Marco. He wasn't about to abandon his charges over his allergy to dominance and pack. Did the asshole have to pull this shit with a fucking audience, though? Why couldn't Adri just have taken over and quietly stopped denying his link to the Lunettis?

A low growl rumbled in his throat as he forced himself to picture the fighters he needed to care for. He wasn't a pack animal. It wasn't in his nature to surround himself with people, but he knew what it was like to lose your family and be alone and untethered in a violent world. He wasn't going to abandon Garett and Finn and all the others, and Jay would never forgive him if he didn't pull his head in on this.

"I'll do it," Adri said, still holding Marco's gaze.

Marco strode closer, and Adri held his ground as the imposing shifter reached out to grab him by his nape, his thumb wrapping around his neck to rub his scent into his skin. Rafe stiffened behind him, but didn't try to stop his Alpha.

"Who do you work for?" Marco asked.

Adri huffed. "You. You made your point, Marco."

Marco's lips stretched in a snarl, and Adri quickly corrected before his jaguar responded to the pissed-off wolf in a way that would get them in trouble. "Fine. You made your point, *Alpha*. Better?"

"And where do you belong?" Marco asked, eyes still glittering with irritatingly smug dominance.

"Here. Whatever," Adri muttered.

The grip on his neck tightened, and Adri rolled his eyes. The asshole wasn't going to give up until he'd got what he wanted. Tipping his head at the slightest angle possible that could still be considered baring his throat, Adri forced his eyes down to Marco's chest, breaking the eye contact standoff they'd been in. Damn wolves and their posturing. A rumbled complaint came from Rafe behind him as Marco leaned in to rub his rough stubble across Adri's neck before stepping back and turning to Silas and carrying on their meeting as if he hadn't just turned Adri's world on its head.

Adri's nose wrinkled as he smelled Marco's scent layered with his own. Sensing his discomfort, Rafe nuzzled in close, and Adri let his head fall further to the side, exposing more of his neck.

"You did good," Rafe murmured, his teeth and lips working over his throat until Marco's scent was half-buried beneath his own and Adri's cock was throbbing in his pants.

Mortification filled him as, instead of telling the doc to shut up like he wanted to, a rumbling purr started vibrating his chest and he butted his head under Rafe's chin as his cat's instincts overrode his better judgement.

Fuck, his jaguar could be a slut for it sometimes. Adri had lost track of the conversation in the chaos of his thoughts and Rafe's possessiveness. He tuned back in as the discussion lulled and looked up to find he was once again the centre of attention as knowing eyes took in his position—basically putty in his mate's arms. Fuck it. If he wanted to be affectionate, he could be. Didn't mean he wouldn't lash out the next time someone got on his nerves.

"I'm glad I got to see you finally pull your head out of your ass and admit you have a mate before I left," Viviana said.

Adri flipped her off, but still pulled away from Rafe so he could go clasp her hand in farewell. "I'll take good care of them until you're back," he promised.

Viviana shook her head. "They've always been more loyal to you. I'm not going to try and take my job back when I return. It's yours now."

"But you will come back?" Adri asked.

Viviana's eyes flicked to Marco and then back to him before she shrugged. "We'll see."

"Fuck you, Vee," he said, pulling her into a hug.

She snickered into his shirt, squeezing him back, before making her way around the room to say the rest of her farewells.

Adri returned to Rafe as he watched the woman he'd worked with for so many years prepare to disappear from his life. Between her management and Rafe's work behind the scenes, they'd transformed his life from what had been basically slavery to one where he was free to choose, free to help make sure the other young fighters never had to go through the hell he had.

Her eyes found his one last time as she shepherded Leah out the door, understanding and acknowledgement passing between them as the knowledge of his new responsibility settled on his shoulders.

For all his dramatic acceptance of the position, it was weirdly easy for Adri to take over management of the fighting ring. He hadn't been worried about the people side of it. He'd always been deeply involved in coaching and smoothing out the tensions that came with two dozen fighters living in close proximity. It wasn't until he'd taken over Viviana's office that he realised the sneaky shifter had been training him as a successor for years.

Each time she'd asked him to take over dealing with their suppliers for a week because she was going to be away, or take over scheduling and dealing with promoters for a big event because Marco had a more urgent task for her, he'd shrugged and got on with it. It was only now that he could see she'd made sure he was familiar with every aspect of what she did. Taking on the responsibility was like donning the suit he wore to enter the venue of high-profile fights. It looked fancy, but at this point, it was so familiar it had become just another reassuring aspect of his routine. The designer fabric didn't change who he was underneath.

Although now that he thought about it, those suits had always just turned up in his wardrobe when he needed a new one. He'd thought Viviana had been responsible, but as he reviewed the budgets, he couldn't see any allowance for it. His sneaky mate had been dressing him even when they never saw each other, and he was so far gone that the knowledge only made him smile.

Speaking of his mate, Rafe had understood his need to stay at his apartment above the gym with the rest of his people while he figured out his new job. Adri's fighters were stressed by Viviana's disappearance and the recent deaths. There was a huge amount of work to do to try to close any security breaches. Viviana had had Adri to help balance the workload, but he hadn't had time to find anyone to fill the gap his promotion left, which meant he barely slept as he worked around the clock. He'd thought maybe Rafe would come stay with him, but the doc had been caught by his own responsibilities, managing a flurry of clinic appointments before flying to visit a university out of state to get a second opinion on the neural chip Adri had found.

It had been strange not to see Rafe for the last couple of weeks. The regular food deliveries that showed up at his door and the constant stream of text check-ins only exacerbated his jaguar's desperation to smell and touch his mate again. He was all but climbing the walls with the need to make sure Rafe was protected.

Marco and Angelo had reassured him numerous times that they had increased security around the clinic and had people shadowing Rafe 24/7, but it still wasn't enough. No one could watch the doc as well as Adri could. His instincts were screaming at him to drop everything and go to his mate, but he couldn't abandon his fighters, and Rafe's plane wouldn't land back in the city for another three hours anyway.

"Watching the clock isn't going to get him here any faster," Jay teased from the doorway to his office.

Adri rolled his eyes and turned to one of his oldest friends. "I was just timing their drills," he said, gesturing out the mirrored glass towards the last two fighters training in the gym.

Most of their people had long since headed to bed. Rafe was on a red-eye back to New Trinity first thing in the morning, and Adri had been far too keyed up at his impending return to seek out his own bed.

"They finished drills ten minutes ago. They're stretching," Jay pointed out, his sharp vampire fangs flashing in the overhead light as he grinned.

Adri scratched his jaw with his middle finger, flipping off his friend and making him smile even wider.

"You need to catch a couple of hours of rest, and then you need to go meet him at the airport," Jay said.

"I don't have time for that," Adri replied, turning his attention back to the complex scheduling he'd been failing to drag into line. Running a fighting ring across three crime family territories when tensions were so high and you needed to constantly change up your venues to avoid being a soft target for terrorist attacks was no easy task.

"Come on, man. The doc's going to kick my ass if he realises I let you work yourself to the bone. You look like shit. You're wearing yesterday's clothes, and you can barely make your eyes focus from lack of sleep. Get the fuck out of here. The schedule will still be there tomorrow."

Leaning back in his chair, Adri pinched the bridge of his

nose, the relief from closing his eyes almost instant. Maybe Jay was right.

"Fine. But I really don't have time to go out to the airport. We've got a delivery right before he lands."

"I can manage the delivery."

Adri just shook his head. If they weren't under threat, Jay could've handled it, but Adri's jaguar wouldn't rest unless he could eyeball the delivery staff himself. The vampire wasn't usually involved in that side of the business. He wouldn't notice if something was off like Adri would.

"I need to be here."

"Fine. I'll message the doc and tell him to come straight to the gym, then."

Adri bit off another yawn. "He already told me he's cleared his calendar for the next three days. I doubt he's going anywhere else."

Jay came further into the room, pulling him to his feet and shepherding him out toward his apartment. "I'm glad you're finally accepting the bond between you," he said, voice soft like he didn't want to panic him.

Adri huffed. "It's not like I could avoid him forever."

"Didn't stop you trying," Jay pointed out.

"I swear it doesn't mean I'll abandon any of you."

Jay's sharp laugh startled him as they reached the door to his place. "No one ever thought it would mean that except you. No more excuses. No regrets. Lock him down already."

Waving off his friend, Adri staggered off to bed, setting his alarm for two hours later so he'd have plenty of time to shower and get himself more presentable before he dealt with the delivery. He hadn't told his friend the real reason he'd refused to stop working on that schedule, despite it being long past midnight, was that he didn't want any distractions once Rafe returned. He didn't intend to let his mate out of his bed for the rest of the day.

It wasn't his alarm that woke Adri up an hour and a half later.

A concussive boom loud enough to have his jaguar reeling as his eardrums bled had him shooting upright just in time for half his roof to collapse on top of him. If he'd still been lying down, he would've been crushed beneath one of the concrete structural supports. Instead, he took a glancing blow to the head as he rolled for cover, choking on masonry dust. The floor dropped out from beneath his feet as he shifted, sinking into animal instinct and letting his jaguar's enhanced senses minimise the damage they took.

His apartment had been on the top floor of the building, along with Jay and a few others. The rest of his fighters lived on the floor below. When the world finally stopped disintegrating around him, he was pretty sure his bed was now resting at street level, and one of his legs was pinned between shattered construction materials. Somehow, the rest of him had managed to land in a pocket of relative safety, but he couldn't see a thing.

Letting out a sawing roar of anger, Adri dragged his mangled limb clear and scrabbled at the wreckage in the direction he was pretty sure his window had been. He needed *out*. Needed out so he could dive back in to save his people. Needed out so he could rend whoever did this limb from limb and paint the streets with their blood. Needed out so his mate could find him and he could burrow into his scent and finally breathe again.

CHAPTER 14: ADRI

If he hadn't shifted, Adri probably wouldn't have been able to drag himself through the gaps in the haphazardly arranged remains of his building to get clear. The pads of his jaguar's paws were much better able to navigate the uneven surfaces that his bare human feet would have been, but he was pretty sure he'd stood on a shard of glass somewhere that had lodged in his foot. He didn't have time to take it out as he directed the fighters who'd got clear and the neighbours who'd come running to search the wreckage. Their shifter senses at least meant they could hear the muffled breaths and cries for help from within.

A low growl sounded behind him as he hauled a doorframe to the side and threw it behind him. Adri hissed as he twisted on his injured foot to face the noise before Rafe's familiar scent rolled over him like a blanket, right before an actual blanket wrapped around his shoulders.

"I followed a trail of your blood to you, kitten. You couldn't take two minutes to let your body reject whatever's in your foot? Sit the fuck down and let me get it out," Rafe said, grabbing a pair of sweats from a wolf shifter passing by and shoving them at Adri's chest hard enough to make him stumble before pulling him into an embrace so tight he couldn't breathe.

"The pack's here?" Adri asked, finally taking in the collection of SUVs parked around them and Marco's commanding presence talking into a phone in the distance.

"Of course, the pack's here. You're ours, and so is everyone in that building. Now get dressed so you can sit down."

Adri winced again as he pulled the sweats on, a cry of protest leaving his lips as Rafe swept him up into his arms to carry him over to the open boot of his SUV. One of his pack mates offered to help, but Rafe snarled so viciously that the guy just backed away with a smirk before returning to the chaos of the bomb site.

Holy fuck. Someone had bombed the building. Guilt flooded through Adri. How had he failed his people so badly?

"This wasn't your fault," Marco rumbled, reaching out to grip his nape firmly as Rafe dropped to a crouch with a torch gripped between his teeth and medical tweezers in hand to sort his foot out. *How had the Alpha snuck up on him?*

"You're still healing a concussion from whatever fell on you," Rafe growled, his hands soft and gentle in sharp contrast to the anger in his voice as he pulled a sliver of glass free. Apparently, he'd said that thought aloud.

"Breathe, Doc. He's safe," Marco said.

"I wasn't here when he needed me," Rafe shot back.

Dropping the glass into a bin, Rafe held a towel to his foot as he felt his shifter healing finally knitting the skin back together. It was only a small injury. If he hadn't been scrabbling around in the rubble and continually pushing it back in, it would've healed immediately.

"I'm okay, Rafe," Adri said, tugging the doc closer by his waist.

"The smell of your blood trailed all over the ground is driving my wolf crazy," Rafe said, burrowing his nose into Adri's neck and biting down hard enough to bruise.

Adri's eyes rolled back as pleasure shot through him. "Gonna make me bleed some more, Doc?"

"This isn't the time or place," Marco said, voice teasing as he reminded them he was still standing right there. "Use your magic to make that mark stick for long enough to calm your wolf down and find your kitten some boots so we can get this sorted."

Adri's groan deepened as the suction on his neck grew deeper and the familiar tingle of Rafe's moonlit magic bit deep into his skin. Marco squeezed his shoulder one last time and stepped away, adjusting his pants as he went. Rafe huffed in annoyance, and Adri turned his head to nuzzle into him, pressing biting kisses across his lips before sucking a hickey into his neck in return. A low chuckle left him as he realised Rafe was using his magic to make that one stick as well.

"What is it with wolves and marking people up?"

"You're *mine*. Everyone needs to know it," Rafe growled, kneeling to put socks and boots on Adri's feet.

"I can do that, Doc," Adri said.

"Just give me thirty more seconds to touch you. To reassure my wolf you're alive," Rafe whispered.

Adri ran his fingers through Rafe's salt-and-pepper hair where he knelt, his other hand reaching up to press at the dull ache where Rafe had bruised his neck. The sensation went straight to his cock, making him shift uncomfortably where he sat as it hardened even further.

Finished with his boots, Rafe turned his head to nose at his erection through his sweats, making Adri groan again.

The moment was broken by a call from the building behind them.

"Doc! We need you!"

Their thirty-second bubble was over. Jumping down from the car, Adri's grim focus returned as he shadowed Rafe back toward the chaos. His people needed them.

Five people. Five fighters he'd trained from the first day they'd stepped foot in the gym and bullied into resting when they were tired. Friends. *Family*. All missing.

They weren't dead. Between shifter senses and witch magic, the pack had thoroughly searched the rubble of the building once they'd cleared the trapped and injured. Thanks to supernatural healing, no one had died in the attack. Yet. But the likelihood that someone was digging around in his people's brains, inserting foreign objects that would turn them feral, while they stood around staring over Luca's shoulder as he hacked into every camera he could find within five blocks of the site was high.

"We'll find them," Rafe promised, wrapping his arms around him from behind.

Adri allowed himself a moment to rest his head back on Rafe's shoulder. The doc had been busy dealing with a raft of injuries. It was true no one had died, but Jay had taken longer than Adri could stand to regain consciousness, one of their newer fighters had lost their leg below the knee, and another's arm had been crushed so badly it had taken Rafe hours of meticulous work with magic and surgery to make sure it healed right as he slowed down the shifter's natural healing so he could rearrange the bones into their proper positions.

"You've worn yourself out again. You should be resting,"

Adri murmured, turning to press a kiss to his neck. Rafe had been right. Life was too fragile, even for shifters. After the trauma of the evening, he was done resisting this thing between them.

"Only if you come rest with me."

"I'll rest when we find them," Adri said.

"That might take a while," Luca said, voice tense with frustration. "I can see them collecting the bodies of anyone they could reach right after the blast, but the trail just disappears in a blind spot a few blocks away. It's like magic, but there's no sign of a witch with them, and Rocco and Cal couldn't sense any residue or power signature when they searched the area. That theory about a tunnel system under the city is sounding more and more likely, although how they've kept it hidden from us all these years is a mystery."

"I might know something about that," Leah said, her voice emerging from the laptop where she and Viviana had called into this meeting from wherever they were holed up.

"Explain," Marco ordered, a growl entering his voice as he glared at the screen.

"I researched the city in the old Council archives in the capital before I was deployed there. The records that hadn't been digitised," Leah said. "I majored in history, so I probably poked around more than most people would. I found an old map from just after the last shifter wars. It showed a series of tunnels and underground chambers that stretched across the central city. When I asked the regional councillor about it, she said it was a plan for subway construction that was never funded, but the layout made no sense for that. It was too tightly contained in the middle of the city, and the chambers were too close together to be of any use as subway stations. It also had witch sigils marked at each exit and a depiction of a massive stone formation of some kind near Central Park."

Rocco straightened from where he'd been leaning against

a wall, checking his phone. "Did it show a connection between the central stone and the sigils? Do you remember the pattern?"

Leah shrugged. "I only got a quick look. I didn't get a chance to take a photo before the councillor took it off me. In retrospect, I think I must've triggered a silent alarm in the archives with how fast she appeared. The only other thing I remember is the label of the map. It read: *Founding Agreement Human Bilateral*."

"I thought the New Trinity Founding Agreement was a tripartite between the three crime families. The humans weren't involved," Rafe said.

"So did I, and I signed the damn thing," Marco added. "What are you thinking, Rocco?"

"There are a few all-supernatural cities in the world that operate within self-sustaining magical shielding that keeps them hidden. The last magic user capable of creating that kind of shield died years ago, but the thing they all have in common is the use of pieces of a specific, unique meteorite to anchor and store the power so that it's not reliant on a witch to permanently maintain it. No one has found an Earth-produced mineral that can perform the same, so they are extremely limited. The properties of the meteorite make it all but impossible for magical searches to pick up its presence."

"So, they have a permanent magical shield under the city? That would explain why we keep losing them," Luca said.

"Can they do anything else with the store of power? Is it just for shielding, or can they channel it into something else?" Marco asked.

"I don't know. The cases I studied were shielding entire above-ground cities from discovery. There wasn't any power spare to do anything more. This one would only need to screen the exit points from casual view. Just the proximity of the meteorite would hide the rest from magical inspection. If they had enough time and expertise, they may well be able to do more with the power source."

"The kind of time and expertise it takes to develop a neural chip that interferes with shifter magic?" Adri asked. He had a really bad feeling about where this was going.

"Yeah, just like that," Rocco replied. "I need to let the MC know about this and see if anyone knows anything more."

"So, just to be clear, the Supernatural Council you're all so careful not to piss off has given a terrorist organisation access to an uncontrolled power supply and hidden pathways across the city?" Adri asked.

"It would have been a concession to reassure the humans who became aware of our existence during the wars. A way to make them feel safer. It's possible the people dealing with the D-2S threat at the Council aren't talking to the people who are aware of the historical arrangement with the humans," Leah said.

Adri rolled his eyes. Fucking bureaucrats.

"Perhaps. But it's more likely someone in the Council is corrupt," Marco said, voice low and dangerous.

Leah tipped her head in acknowledgement. "Yes and no. It may not even be a question of corruption. If there is an active risk of exposure of our kind, the Council can justify almost anything. The D-2S is only targeting New Trinity City right now, whereas an exposure event could affect the entire world. Once our existence gets out, there's no going back."

"You're saying the Council could be catering to the terrorists?" Rafe asked.

"If they are, they would keep that information tightly contained. Their power is dependent on the trust of the supernatural community. It's a delicate balance. They probably think if they bide their time, they'll get an opportunity to take them out."

"Do you think the mayor and police chief are involved?

The Council has always limited their human communications to those two," Silas said.

"As far as we know," Luca muttered.

"If they are, they're dead. I can't tolerate support for supernatural terrorists, and I doubt the other families would either. The Council can find new humans to dance to their tune," Marco said.

"When's the next time you'll see them? You don't want to tip them off with an unusual meeting," Leah said.

Marco glanced over at Adri, and he straightened from where he was pressed into Rafe's chest. "There's a charity fight at the hospital in a couple of weeks. They'll definitely be there," the Alpha said.

"I can sound them out," Adri offered, sparking a sharp nip at his neck from his mate.

"*We* can sound them out," Rafe corrected. "As a pack."

"I was already planning to attend," Marco agreed.

"I'll sort a security plan and extra coverage," Angelo said. "Although without the details of where these tunnel entrances are, I can't guarantee we can corner them."

"They're human. They can only run so fast," Marco growled.

Strong fingers dug into Adri's shoulder muscles as he hunched over his computer, and he suppressed a groan as he leaned back into Rafe's touch.

"I don't care what you were planning. You owe the pack. You're not kicking my guys out," Adri growled into the phone.

The scramble between finding places for his people to stay, rescheduling upcoming fights because of missing fighters, and searching the streets for any sign of them any chance he got meant he hadn't paid as much attention to his emails as he should. Otherwise, he would've noticed this asshole was trying to back out on his commitment to Marco earlier.

The owner of the hostel snivelled something about going over his head, and Adri laughed.

"Go ahead. Try bothering Alpha Lunetti with this and see how much patience he has for people who go back on their word against his interests."

"There's a fucking vampire in my building, and you're a damn cat. I didn't sign up for this shit."

Rafe was vibrating with anger behind him, and Adri twisted so his protective mate couldn't reach to grab the phone from his hand. To his credit, Rafe managed to hold himself back, but Adri could tell it was a near thing. He could also tell the doc was texting someone about what he'd just heard—probably Silas. This guy would be lucky to make it through the night. He hadn't needed Rafe to jump in, and he proved it by bullying the guy into doing what he wanted before hanging up.

"I had it covered," Adri snapped, letting his head fall back with a moan as Rafe continued to knead his tense muscles.

Rafe took advantage of the new angle to claim his lips in a kiss, and Adri let himself forget the mountain of tasks waiting for him for a few seconds as he sank into it.

"He took it too far. He needs a reminder that his loyalty to the pack isn't a subscription he can fucking cancel. Marco has no tolerance for that kind of talk, especially after what happened with Gio. Your job is to make the fighting ring successful. Silas' is to keep people like him in line. You're part of a pack. You don't have to do it all alone."

Adri sighed and pressed his fingers to his temple as Rafe spun his office chair so they were facing each other.

"When was the last time you got a good night's sleep, kitten?"

Adri looked away from Rafe's piercing inspection and shrugged. The doc already knew the answer, so there was no point in lying. Rafe had shadowed his every move whenever he wasn't busy with his own work. He'd probably had even less sleep than Adri.

That thought had him looking back up at Rafe as his forehead furrowed in concern. The doc had dark circles under his eyes, and his skin was paler than it should be.

"I could ask you the same," Adri said.

"Come on. It's the full moon. We're going to go run for a reason other than chasing down terrorists until we're too tired to keep going and then get at least four hours' sleep before we go back to work," Rafe said, pulling Adri to his feet and into his arms.

Adri couldn't resist the urge to nuzzle into the base of his neck as Rafe held him close, drawing in deep breaths of his scent.

"I don't have time for that," Adri said, but there was no force in his words.

"Alpha's orders," Rafe said.

Adri stiffened as his jaguar snarled inside him at the suggestion that someone was telling him what to do or where to go.

"Hush, kitten. You wouldn't want me running in the forest alone, would you?"

"I know what you're doing," Adri complained as his jaguar flipped from fuming to focussed on their mate in less time than it took for him to draw in another heady breath.

"Enticing my mate into fucking under the open sky?"

Adri's cock swelled so fast it ached, and he bit down hard on Rafe's collarbone before spinning him to press him up against the wall so he could taste every inch of his throat with rasping kitten licks. A smirk stretched his mouth as Rafe drew in a sharp inhalation of surprise before gripping his hips hard enough to bruise and grinding them together.

"What's wrong with fucking on my desk?" Adri whispered.

Rafe reached up and wrapped a hand around his throat, squeezing just hard enough to make him feel thoroughly owned without triggering a defensive response.

"Let me take care of you, kitten."

Huffing out a breath, Adri pulled back. "Fine."

They were some of the last to arrive at the pack lands. The braziers on the grass beside the edge of the forest were mostly surrounded by the very young or old, watched over by a few of Angelo's enforcers, along with Marco, Vin, and Rocco. The Alpha's eyes flashed with satisfaction at their presence as they approached, but Adri kept his contrary annoyance to himself. He didn't fancy getting smacked into the dirt when he was already exhausted and running on fumes.

"Not running with your mates tonight?" Rafe asked the vampire and the witch standing nearby.

"We'll watch over the house until everyone's back," Rocco replied.

"Come run with me," Marco said, stripping off his shirt.

"You made your point about where I belong already," Adri huffed, tugging his clothes off with more force than was necessary and ignoring the satisfied smiles passing between his mate and his Alpha.

"Hearing it and feeling it aren't the same thing," Marco replied right before he shifted into a huge black Alpha wolf that was intimidating as fuck.

Rafe grabbed his nape, pressing a hard kiss to his lips before shifting as well. Adri took a deep, silent breath and let his jaguar take over, sinking into the sensation of his muscles and bones transforming.

Rafe was still taller than him in this form, but not as solid. His silver and black fur reminded Adri of the sexy silver Daddy vibes his mate had going on as a human. With his instincts riding him so much harder in this body, Adri butted his head up under Rafe's chin, a soft purr vibrating in his chest as Rafe softly bit down on his ear in response.

Marco slunk closer as they pressed against each other, his looming presence pure dominance. Twisting to face him while still pressing into his mate's side, Adri let the Alpha press their muzzles together briefly before rubbing his face along Adri's, scenting him. Rafe's wolf let out a low grumble of complaint, but quickly tipped his head in submission as Marco gave him the same treatment.

Throwing his head back, Marco let out a long, loud howl to the moon above them, his body focussed on the forest beyond them as, one by one, their packmates out running responded to the call until a symphony of connection sang into the night. Adri couldn't howl, but he added his jaguar's roar to the mix before dropping his head low to tear into the forest, catching his mate by surprise.

Rafe and Marco's amused yips followed close behind him as they tracked him into the forest, especially when he took the first chance he could get to bunch his muscles under him and launch himself up one of the thick tree trunks and into the canopy. He'd always preferred to stalk at height. The trees were close enough here that he'd be able to keep an eye on the wolves from above as they moved through the forest, so long as they didn't try to run all-out.

As they made their way into the darkness, his jaguar became more playful, dropping down from above unexpectedly as Rafe and Marco ran together and slipping off into the shadows before they had a chance to do more than brush against him. The cat side of himself was having the time of its life. The human side was wondering if he'd ever live this down.

Eventually, Marco caught him in one of his ambushes, twisting to bite gently on Adri's scruff and using his head to nudge him at Rafe before running off to connect with the rest of his pack. Adri twined himself around his mate as Rafe used his long tongue to lick at the places Marco had touched him, covering his scent with his own.

Adri's eyes slipped closed as he indulged in Rafe's touch, and he didn't immediately notice when tongue and muzzle changed to human fingers stroking through his fur.

"You're so beautiful like this, kitten," Rafe murmured.

Lifting his head from where it was resting on his paws, Adri blinked up at him. They'd stopped on the edge of a small lake, the water glinting in the moonlight and soft grasses rustling quietly beneath them. Stretching deeply in a move that made his back arch and his tail lash, Adri let the shift take him.

A low groan escaped Rafe from behind him as he continued to stretch in his human form—his chest brushing against the ground as his hips stayed high. He wasn't presenting to his mate. He was just being very dedicated to his flexibility.

"If you stay like that, you know exactly how we're going to end up," Rafe growled, his voice dropping an octave as his hand brushed down the curve of Adri's ass to his muscled thighs.

"Can you do it without biting and knotting me?" Adri asked.

A pained moan left Rafe as he leaned in close, pressing a kiss to Adri's tailbone. Adri's arch grew even more pronounced as he tried to entice those lips lower.

"There's no way I can control myself when you're like

this," Rafe said, his tongue slipping out to circle Adri's aching hole like he was about to make a whole fucking meal of it.

Hissing in annoyance at himself for denying them both, Adri flopped onto his back, the move taking him out of reach of that clever tongue.

"I can't," he said.

Rafe's eyes shone gold in the night, and Adri's gaze traced down the veins of his arms to his fisted hands, but none of the tension thrumming through his body was audible in his voice when he spoke.

"Okay, kitten. Whenever you're ready."

"You have the patience of a saint."

Rafe shrugged. "I want you willing, or not at all."

Adri groaned and threw his arm over his eyes to hide the view of his mate before he jumped him. "I'm plenty willing. I just can't. Not yet. Not until we find them."

"You don't have to earn your happiness, kitten. You deserve it all."

"I can't take our forever while five of the people I'm responsible for might be about to have theirs cut short."

"So, we find them. Together. Now shift back so we don't get hypothermia sleeping out here."

Adri's jaguar was slow to emerge as he shifted, reluctant to give up on the potential mate bond he was denying.

Once he was settled in jaguar form, Rafe wrapped human arms around him for a moment, whispering in his ear before shifting to his wolf—"Our forever is here already, kitten. Whether we ever complete the bond or not. I will always be here for you."

CHAPTER 15: RAFE

The glittery hospital fundraiser was about as far as you could get from waking up in the forest in wolf form still wrapped around your mate. The tux Adri was sporting as they arrived at the Town Hall for the evening's *'civilised'* violence was just begging to be stripped off him with the way it emphasised every muscled inch of his body.

A wave of satisfaction washed through him as Rafe spied the bruise in the shape of his teeth that was peeking out above Adri's collar. He'd made sure to refresh it each day and keep it from healing with his power. It was the only way to keep his wolf from becoming frantic with the need to complete the bond.

"They really went all out with the Valentine's theme," Adri observed as they paused in the entryway to take in the metallic red and pink explosion of the space. "I liked Emmy's decorations better."

Rafe laughed and pressed a kiss to Adri's temple. Emmy's version of a fighting ring from the ill-fated bout where Adri had almost lost his arm had involved dead bodies hanging from the ceiling. But artistically, it had certainly been more sophisticated.

"This has its charm."

"Adri! You made it! It's so nice to meet you in person at last," Katie called, pulling him into an embrace before air-kissing his cheeks.

"Wouldn't miss it," Adri said, eyeing the temporary fighting ring that was centre stage in the room. "Tell me the safety gear you arranged isn't also covered in glitter?"

"I couldn't possibly comment," Katie said with a smile.

Rafe smirked as he leaned in to greet his friend's wife. She had a wicked sense of humour, so the chances Adri would end up with sparkly bubble-gum-pink, or worse, gloves and head protection were high. It's not like he had his own gear to use. Shifters didn't bother for obvious reasons.

"Ah! The guest of honour has arrived!" a voice called.

Rafe and Adri turned as one to face the new arrival. Rafe wrapped a protective arm around Adri's waist, angling himself so the mayor approaching with a wide smile would have to go through him to get to his mate. Adri huffed an annoyed breath against his throat but let him get away with it as they both worked to act casual while greeting one of the men they suspected had been hiding terrorists beneath their very feet.

It seemed unlikely the mayor wasn't involved if the tunnel system was part of the Council's arrangement with the few humans who were aware of supernaturals in the city. They needed proof before they could act on something that would destabilise the peace of the city so massively, though. There was always the chance the mayor was another victim who'd been forced to dance to the D-2S's tune.

Nothing about the calculated look the mayor gave them as he took in Rafe's protective stance suggested he was concerned for his safety. He was in full mayoral regalia for the evening, his gold chains of office hanging large and gaudy around his neck.

"It's good to see you, Stewart," Rafe said, reaching out to shake the mayor's hand and squeezing just a little too hard for a human as he purposefully avoided using his title.

"Always a pleasure, Doc. Where's your boss hiding this evening?"

Rafe reached up to give his mate's nape a calming squeeze as Adri responded with a low growl to the mayor's words. They were innocuous enough if they'd been human, but Stewart had enough experience in their world to know the suggestion that an Alpha was hiding from him was skirting the lines of politeness.

"I think the better question is where you've been hiding? Or *what*?" Adri said.

Rafe's smirk grew wider. It wasn't the most subtle approach, but there was something to be said for testing the mayor's reaction to this kind of question. Stewart had been in politics long enough that his face remained relaxed as he pretended to laugh at the question, but Rafe heard the slight increase in his heart rate and saw the tension in his muscles as the human resisted his fight-or-flight response to being questioned by two predators. It wasn't conclusive, but Rafe was pretty sure he was hiding something. Luca had turned as much of his attention to the mayor and chief of police as he could afford to divert from the D-2S, so it was only a matter of time before they'd have a lead.

"Thank you so much for the donation from your office, Your Worship," Katie said, cutting through the weird tension between them with practised diplomacy. "Maybe we'll get you into the ring next year?"

Stewart laughed again. "I'm too old to be bouncing around, throwing punches. I'll leave that to the young things who don't know any better," he replied, his eyes flicking back to Adri.

Marco stepped up next to Rafe as he stared down the mayor, trying to decide if the hidden insult to his mate in his words was worth responding to.

"We both know the young don't have a monopoly on ill-advised activities that might lead them to an early grave," Marco said, baring too-sharp fangs in a smile as he reached out to shake the mayor's hand in greeting.

Tension coiled inside him as Marco held on a second too long, refusing to relinquish Stewart's hand until the mayor broke eye contact. The delicate balance of the city felt poised on the precipice, threatening to fall at any moment.

Adri leaned in close as they moved away to let the two men face off. "You good here? I need to go help prepare the fighters backstage."

Rafe smiled at the hint of disgust in his mate's voice. Adri hadn't whispered a word of complaint about helping Katie out with the night when she'd asked, but babysitting inexperienced human fighters for a fundraiser definitely wasn't his idea of a good time.

"You're the best, kitten. I'll make it up to you later tonight," Rafe murmured back, letting the room fade from his awareness for a second as he sank into the constant heat between them.

"You better," Adri said, pressing a brief kiss to his lips before pulling away.

Rafe reached out to grasp his nape before he could leave, tugging him back in for a deeper kiss that had them both breathing harder. Unable to resist the temptation of the bruise he'd been refreshing every day on Adri's neck, Rafe leaned in to mouth at it, sucking hard and biting down, all but gnawing at his mate as he used his power to make the deep impressions of his teeth remain long after his mate walked away.

"Doc," Adri moaned in complaint. "You're going to make me..."

Drawing on a bit more of his power, Rafe pulled back and smiled at Adri as he used it to stop the blood trying to fill out his mate's cock as he responded to Rafe's attention.

Adri's moan turned into a whine of complaint, and Rafe raised an eyebrow. "You didn't want to cross the room like that, did you?"

Adri huffed. "Do you have *any* idea how much worse that's making my frustration?"

"You're so beautiful like this. Aching for me to control your pleasure."

Rafe patted his chest soothingly, sliding his hand under Adri's tux jacket that he'd left open and letting his fingers brush over his mate's hard nipples through his shirt. Adri tipped his head back to stare at the ceiling, tension in every line of his body, but he didn't tell him to stop.

"Have you had enough fun now? I need to go get ready."

When Rafe finally released Adri, he couldn't tear his eyes from his mate's body as he moved smoothly through the ballroom toward the backstage area where the fighters were gathering. Blinking as he came back to himself, Rafe realised Stewart had left while he was distracted.

"You've got it bad, Doc," Marco teased.

"I assure you it is very, very good."

A flash of yearning crossed Marco's face before the Alpha's social mask descended once more.

"Sorry," Rafe murmured, knowing how hard it was for Marco to watch his family and pack finding their mates when his own had died in his arms when he was just a teenager.

"Don't be sorry for that. Don't hide it. Hold on and don't ever let go."

Rafe and Katie exchanged a look, and she deftly changed the subject, drawing a laugh out of their Alpha with her quiet, wicked commentary on her colleagues and the city's dignitaries gathered for the event.

Adri wasn't scheduled for the first couple of fights, and the shifters quickly grew bored with watching humans throw slow, weak punches at each other before giving up far too soon.

"When's your kitten coming out? At least then we'll have something pretty to look at," Marco grumbled under his breath.

"Watch it, Alpha," Rafe warned, sparking another laugh from Marco. At least he seemed over his maudlin moment. "Did we get what we needed on the mayor and police chief?"

"I haven't seen the chief. I put one of our trackers on Stewart while we were talking, though. Hopefully, it stays on long enough for Luca to catch him."

"Something was off about him tonight."

"Agreed. He's forgotten who put him in that role and how easy it would be to take it away."

Rafe's attention shifted back to the fighting ring as the emcee for the night announced Adri's first bout. A sense of wrongness shot down his spine as one of the ushers hurried out from the backstage area, whispering in the emcee's ear.

To his left, Marco was already on his phone, asking for a report from Luca and Angelo. Rafe didn't need to tear his gaze away from searching the crowded room to know something was very wrong. Katie's expression as she moved too fast through the surrounding humans said it all.

"Where is he?" Rafe snapped, barely keeping his wolf under control as he snarled inside him, begging to be let free to hunt and kill.

"He's gone."

CHAPTER 16: ADRI

Something wasn't right. Adri lay absolutely still as he tried to process. Cold metal beneath his naked skin. The scent of damp and city grime in his nose. He tried an experimental move of his hand only to find it couldn't respond as some kind of restraint tugged at his wrist. When he let his eyes peek open the tiniest amount, pitch blackness met his vision. The kind of darkness even his jaguar eyes couldn't make sense of.

Swallowing down a rumbling growl, he tried to figure out if shifting was going to make this better or worse. Changing forms while restrained could be a recipe for dislocated and broken limbs if you weren't careful. Those would heal, though. It was more important that he got free before whoever had left him there returned.

Reaching for his jaguar, Adri willed his bones and muscles to transform. It was only then that he noticed the ever-present awareness of his animal side in his mind was silent. His breaths started coming faster, too fast, and he forced himself to slow the frantic rise and fall of his chest. Calm. He needed to stay calm. It was easier said than done when he couldn't even fully inhale against the tight band pinning him down to the metal table. Even worse, he had a sinking suspicion it wasn't a table at all, but a gurney.

Everything Rafe had told him about his suspicions about the D-2S's medical experimentation ran through Adri's mind in a flurry of panicked thoughts. He gave up his attempt to hide his return to consciousness and strained against the metal and leather holding him in place, using every bit of his strength. Frantic.

Whoever had secured him had done it well. There wasn't the slightest give that he could leverage, and his muscles felt lethargic. Lacking. Now that he was focussed on the physical sensations he usually ignored as fleeting inconveniences to his supernatural healing, the sharp throbbing in his head like he'd never experienced became overwhelming. The flex of his muscles against the restraints made him aware of another dull ache in the crook of his elbow, where he could feel fiery liquid flowing into his veins faster as his blood started rushing. A cannula of some kind. The burn of the drug was a constant irritation that only panicked him more. What the fuck were they pumping into his body?

The click of a lock was like a gunshot in the silent room as Adri strained to escape, eyes wide and teeth bared—teeth, not fangs, because he still couldn't reach his jaguar. When bright white light flooded the room, he winced and fought the urge to squeeze his eyes closed, tears streaming down his cheeks in response to the pain as he focussed his attention on the three people entering. Three *humans*.

"Good. He's awake," a man in a white coat said.

"Looks like you've finally cracked it. We haven't had one die from shock in over a month," another replied.

"What the fuck did you do to me?" Adri asked, voice rasping.

The men ignored him.

"How long until it takes effect?" A more familiar voice asked, someone Adri couldn't quite crane his neck far enough to view. Was that the *mayor*? That answered the question of how high up the terrorist rot went in the city's governance.

"The chip is already rewiring his brain. Generally, susceptibility comes at around days three to five, and any unfortunate side effects emerge by day ten."

Susceptibility to *what*? Ferality? Or was that the unfortunate side effect?

Stewart stepped closer, finally entering Adri's field of vision.

"What the fuck is this?"

Adri tried to snap at the mayor's fingers with blunt teeth as he reached out to grab his jaw and tilt his head to the side, but he was still too lethargic and weak to resist. He *hated* that. Hated being vulnerable. Hated being confined again. It took everything he had not to start hyperventilating as he forced himself to focus on a single trail of stains on the concrete ceiling. It was earthy and damp, suggesting he was somewhere in the tunnel system under the city. He pretended the stain was arterial blood spatter, letting his mind drift in a fantasy where he ripped himself free of his restraints and slashed this asshole's throat with his claws.

"It's just a bruise," one of the scientists muttered, distracting Adri from his thoughts.

"He's a fucking shifter. They don't bruise like this. Who did this to you?" Stewart asked, wrenching Adri's face around to look at him.

Glaring up at the mayor with what he knew was a reckless grin, Adri decided to see how much he could mess with the humans. "My *mate*. He's going to fucking disembowel you and string you from the ceiling by your guts. He's good at that because he's a doctor. A *real* one. Not like these wannabe evil scientists you've got going on."

"You were refusing to complete the bond. The other fighters we took confirmed it," Stewart said, a hint of real fear seeping into his voice.

"How come I've got an unhealed bite mark on my neck, then?" Adri asked, hoping they didn't look close enough to realise the teeth marks had never broken the skin.

"*Fuck!* We can't risk exposure of this location. We need to move him now!"

Adri smirked as he smelled terror and weakness in the air, despite the absence of his jaguar from his mind. This was his chance to maximise the likelihood that his people would be found. "You need to move *all* of us. My Alpha isn't going to leave our fighters behind, and my mate will already have locked in on the location."

Chaos ensued as Stewart and the head scientist started barking orders, a flurry of more humans descending around them.

"We need to move him *now* and hope they haven't managed to map his location yet. The shielding on the entrances won't stop them from digging down to us."

"Get the Sabatini warehouse cleared. We'll put all the pack's people there and draw them away from the tunnels. If they get their people back, they won't be able to justify a further attack to the Council, and the magic needed to break through our defences is too much to hide from them. Move the rest of our forces back to the blue district so we can collapse the tunnels here if they're breached."

"Shall we terminate the subjects before we move them?"

Adri's blood ran cold. Once again, he tried and failed to tear himself free of his restraints.

"Not yet. By the time the pack finds them, they'll either be feral or under our control. Either way, they should be able to take some of them out. We can always detonate the chips remotely if we need to," Stewart said. "Knock him out again so we don't have any more fuck ups."

Adri snarled at the scientist who stepped close to mess with his IV line, and the human looked down at him with derision. "I'm going to put you down like the animal you are as soon as I get the word."

"I'm going to get my mate to keep you alive and conscious with his power while my pack tears you into pieces as tiny as your small-minded fucking brain."

"I wouldn't be making threats about my brain in your position. That chip you have in yours is controlled by an app on my phone."

Unconsciousness pulled at him, and Adri's vision darkened as whatever this asshole had inserted into his IV started to take effect. The human's last retort followed him down into oblivion.

"Sweet dreams, asshole. If you wake up, you'll be nothing more than another weapon. With any luck, you'll kill that mate of yours for us."

CHAPTER 17: RAFE

"Are you sure this guy is trustworthy?" Rafe asked, knowing he'd been driving Emmy up the wall the entire drive with his questions.

It wasn't Rafe's fault. It had been two fucking *days* since his mate went missing. Two days with no sleep. Two days of his wolf howling non-stop inside him. Two days of feeling like his heart had been ripped in two and his soul was stretched tight enough to shatter.

"Seth's young, but he's good people. His tips have always been solid, and he hates vampires as much as we do."

"He *is* a vampire," Rafe pointed out.

"He's a vampire who was turned against his will and pimped out to the scum of the city. He'd take down Kyan and the whole coven without batting an eye if he had the power and connections to do it."

"How young are we talking?"

"Twenty-five. He must've been turned in the last three years or so because he's still figuring out what he's capable of. His control is shaky."

"And why is he willing to give us the time of day? I

would've thought he'd hate all supernaturals with a history like his."

"He's definitely wary of us, so don't go all alpha-Dom on him. I helped him out with a problem he was having. We had a bonding moment."

Rafe's mouth twitched in as much of a smile as he could manage right then. "Why do I feel like your bonding moment involved bondage and blood?"

"Because you know me?"

"Where are we meeting this guy, anyway? Are you just cruising every spot sex workers frequent in the city?" Rafe asked as Emmy slowed down to peer at the shadowy figures leaning against the brickwork in the alley nearby.

"He didn't answer my text. I suspect his pimp confiscated his phone. So, yeah."

Emmy pulled the car into a park. "If he's not here, we might be able to get one of the others to talk," he said, gesturing toward the handful of scantily clad people nearby—a mixture of genders and mostly human, but all with an air of desperation. This wasn't the kind of area someone worked if they had any choice in the matter.

From far away, they looked alluring, but the closer they got, the more signs of illness and abuse Rafe could sense. It was enough to distract his wolf from pining for their mate. They wanted to heal every one of these people and take them home to feed them a hot meal.

"Vampire territory. You can't," Emmy reminded him, sensing the turn of his thoughts.

"I *know* that," Rafe said, teeth gritted in frustration as he watched a young woman nearby hide a shiver. None of them were dressed for the winter weather.

Continuing their search of the dirty streets, they walked briskly so they wouldn't get caught in an interaction with anyone. They'd question these people if they needed to, but it was better if they could leave as little trace as possible of the Lunetti Pack's interest in Emmy's informant.

"Looking for something special, gentlemen?" a soft voice called from nearby.

Emmy spun, a flash of relief crossing his features. "Thank fuck," he murmured, before calling out louder to Seth—"What are you offering, sweet thing?"

Even Rafe's shifter vision struggled to pierce the shadows to see the young vampire as his pupils adjusted from the sharp white glare of the streetlights to the darkened alley he was waiting in. When he finally came into focus, a growl left Rafe's throat.

"What the fuck?"

The young vampire was wearing not much more than a head-to-toe, wide-fishnet body stocking. A scanty metallic jockstrap was the only thing stopping him from flashing them. That wasn't what had caught Rafe's eye, though. He'd never seen a vampire so emaciated. His eyes were sunken in dark shadows like he hadn't slept in weeks, and the lines of bruises stretched around his neck like a collar should never have remained with even a baby vamp's healing ability. Rafe could make out the outline of each thick finger of whoever had choked him out.

"Seth..." Emmy said, his voice trailing off into fuming concern.

The young vampire took one look at their looming worry and looked like he wanted to bolt. Rafe scanned the alleyway behind him, relieved to see it was a dead end. There was no way this guy could outrun them in his current condition.

"What do you want?" Seth hissed, his eyes darting to the street in hypervigilance.

"To get you away from your fucking asshole of a pimp," Emmy snapped. "Get in our car and don't come back."

Seth scoffed. "Yeah, that's not why you came looking for me. Everyone wants something."

Emmy shrugged. "It can be both."

"I can't hide on the pack lands for the rest of my life. I need to earn my place as a vampire with my own kind, and it's not like shifters aren't just as violent." The words sounded like something that had been beaten into him. A refrain from whatever evil fuck had turned him that had eroded at Seth's sense of self until he truly couldn't see any other way out. Rafe had seen it before. Too many times. It also sounded like the coven had seeded some pre-emptive messages about the other supernaturals to ensure Seth didn't go running to the other families for help. The poor guy sounded terrified.

Gripping Emmy's shoulder before he drove Seth away with his need to protect him, Rafe reached for his power. "Let me heal you, at least."

Seth staggered back two steps, panic in his eyes as his voice grew too loud. "No!" Swallowing hard as his eyes kept scanning their surroundings, he murmured the rest of his reply almost too softly for Rafe to make out. "It'll be worse if the marks aren't still there when I go back."

Rafe dropped his arm back to his side, his hands closing into fists. "Fine, but I can at least help with your energy levels."

Stepping forward slowly so he didn't startle the skittish vampire, he reached out to cup his face, running a thumb under those dark bruises beneath his eyes. His power flowed through him without thought. It was all he could do to stop it from healing the poor guy. Instead, he let magic take the place of nutrition and sleep, feeding Seth just enough of his own energy so he would at least be able to run if someone less well-meaning cornered him in an alley later.

"What—oh," Seth said, eyes widening in surprise as he felt the effects of Rafe's magic.

Rafe crossed his arms tight over his chest before he healed too much, forcing his magic back inside his skin. "My clinic is in the neutral zone on the south edge of the ring road. When you need me again, come there. Don't wait."

Seth seemed to shake himself out of his shock, stepping in closer and putting a delicate hand on Rafe's chest above his crossed arms as he blinked up at him. He was so fucking small.

"How can I repay you?"

Nausea twisted in Rafe's gut at the implication that his healing was conditional on *that,* but Emmy's snort from next to him interrupted before he could figure out what to say.

"I told you, we're not like that, Seth. No one wants in your pants, especially Rafe. Chill," Emmy said.

Seth's brow furrowed, like he couldn't quite comprehend the words. "Why *especially Rafe*?"

"He's a healer first. He would never. But he also has a mate who's missing. That's why we came."

Seth nodded, stepping back. "So, you did need something. Did your mate run from you?"

Rafe sighed. It wasn't Seth's fault that he didn't understand shifter culture and assumed the worst. The poor guy would've been raised human and oblivious before the coven turned him and forced him into this life. All he knew of the supernatural community was violence, assault, and whatever lies the coven had fed him.

"No. He was taken from me. Two nights ago. By the terrorist group we've been hunting—the D-2S."

Seth nodded, all focus now. "The tunnels, right? I still haven't managed to catch anyone coming or going, but I know they're there. Tell me about your guy."

Rafe gave a clipped description of Adri, forcing himself to stick to physical appearance and avoid talking about the way his mate's eyes glowed with defiance or the way his face softened when he was mentoring his crew. His words cut off partway through describing the other young fighters who'd been taken as Seth's eyes widened in recognition.

"You've seen something. Tell me," Rafe said, urgency rushing through him.

"You said one of them has dyed green hair? When I'm struggling with my hunger, they make me run circuits in the neighbourhood I stay in to distract me. There's a warehouse on Albertine that's usually vacant, but yesterday there were people there—humans. I didn't see your guy, but there was a flash of green from the loading bay that drew my attention, and I heard them complaining about having to move live shifters. I figured they must've been associated with the coven and I needed to mind my own business, but it was weird they were human. Master Valryn doesn't usually use them for that kind of thing."

"Could you make out anything else? How many? What kind of weapons?" Emmy asked.

"I mean, yeah. It was broad daylight. There were nine of them in three SUVs carrying semiautomatics that I assume were loaded with silver of some kind."

Rafe's jaw dropped as Seth's words distracted him from the vital intel temporarily.

"They make you run during the *day*?"

No wonder the vampire was so exhausted and his injuries weren't healing. He was far too young to spend extended periods out in the sun like that, especially as starved as he was.

Seth shrugged, his face twisting in a subtle wince as he did, and Rafe reached out to spin him around, growling as he took in the whip marks across his shoulders.

"I can't stand for this," Rafe snapped as Seth pulled away, arms wrapped around himself as he dipped his head to stare at the ground.

"It's not your fucking call. I've seen how shifters treat vampires. You're *enemies*. I'm better off where I am," Seth said.

"Who? Tell me which shifter hurt you and I'll end them the same way I ended that asshole who cut you," Emmy growled.

"Good luck finding your mate," Seth muttered, pushing past them.

It took every inch of his control not to stop Seth from leaving, throw him over his shoulder, and take him home, where he could learn that not everyone would hurt him.

"Why the fuck haven't you saved that boy already?" Rafe growled at Emmy as they stalked back to the car.

"You saw him. He doesn't want to be saved. I'm working on it. Building his trust."

"He'll be dead before he has time to trust you."

Emmy stared in the direction Seth had disappeared, concern on his face. "I think you might be right. I'll talk to Marco. See what we can do."

Rafe pinched the bridge of his nose. "If you let Marco get one look at that kid, he'll burn the fucking city down for him." Their Alpha had a type, and Seth would push every fucking one of his buttons.

Emmy smirked. He'd always loved a bit of chaos. "I'm counting on it. Now, let's go save your fucking mate so you don't burn the city down, too."

As much as Rafe was singularly focussed on getting to the warehouse Seth had mentioned, he was grateful they took the time to swing by the pack lands when he saw what Luca had waiting for them.

"I've been studying the chip your mate found us. I didn't have time to isolate exactly what the best countermeasure was, so I've cobbled together something that's part signal blocker, part targeted EMP. It's running off a generator at the moment, so it's pretty unwieldy, but it will fit in the back of one of the SUVs. The closer you can get it to the chips, the better."

Rafe watched as the pack loaded him up. He'd already made sure he had everything he needed for an emergency field surgery within hours of realising Adri was missing. He wasn't going to take any chances. Katie was on call to talk him through it if it came to that. He hoped it didn't. Brain surgery in those kinds of conditions was dangerous even for a shifter. Rafe would need every shred of his power to keep his patients alive, and at the same time, he'd be the one wielding the scalpel. Luca's mate, Cal, had slipped him two vials of the stimulant the witch used when he needed to use power past his capacity. They'd have to hope it was enough.

"Weren't we just fucking here?" Silas muttered as the SUVs pulled up out of sight of the building they were approaching.

"How many warehouses in vampire territory have we had to raid now? It can't be a coincidence," Emmy replied.

"Yeah, I'm pretty fucking over it as well. Keep an eye out for anything we can tie to Kyan or the coven," Marco said, leaning against the side of a car as he did something on his phone while they waited for their scouts to return and tell them if the building was rigged with explosives.

They weren't taking any chances this time. Four witches and a wolf were checking each side of the building.

"What's the plan?" Rafe asked, eyes trained in the direction of the building and nostrils flaring as he drew in deep breaths of the cold night air, trying to catch his mate's scent on the breeze.

Luca's voice came through softly from the speaker on Marco's phone. The hacker was at the pack house with his mate, where he had a better set-up to provide surveillance. "Drive the SUV with the signal blocker straight through the doors and hope it works so they can't trigger the chips."

"That's it? What if it hits my mate?"

"He'll recover from broken bones. He might not recover from whatever that chip is doing," Marco said.

A shiver of rage rocked Rafe's body. The world faded away as the reality he'd been so pointedly ignoring so he could function rocked him to his core. He didn't even hear his Alpha's voice as he darted to the SUV with the blocker, flipped the generator switch, and slid behind the wheel. Didn't hear the curses as his pack scrambled to come in behind him in support. All he could think about was Adri somewhere in that building. Of the filthy technology that had probably violated his mate's brain. Of what he would do if he lost his mate before they could even bond.

Eyes glowing, fangs lengthening, and claws digging into the leather of the steering wheel, Rafe slammed his foot on the accelerator so hard the whole car skidded out as he shot forward, and he was forced to wrestle it back into submission. He barely processed the blur of motion as he sped down the street, heading straight for the loading doors Seth had described.

His shoe was still flat to the floor when he made contact. Wood splintered away from him into the dark void ahead as he spun the wheel, pulled the hand brake, and wrenched the car to a stop. His desperation to get to his mate as quickly as possible was almost his undoing—the SUV tilting onto its side and almost overbalancing as his momentum had nowhere to go. He'd be fine if the SUV crashed out, but his medical supplies might not be, and they'd take more time to access. Thankfully, he'd executed it perfectly, the wheels of the vehicle reconnecting with the concrete floor in a dusty thump as the rest of the pack ran in through the hole in the wall he'd just made.

Shoving the door open hard enough to rip it off its hinges, Rafe tore from the vehicle, head turning as he hunted the jungle scent that had been haunting his memories for days.

"Fucking hell, Doc. A little warning would've been—" Silas' words cut off with a curse as a figure slammed into him from behind, tackling him to the ground.

Red eyes flashed in the darkness as Silas twisted to throw the guy clear.

"Fuck. He's feral! Contain him or kill him, but don't let him get his fucking teeth in you," Marco snapped.

A strangled howl broke from Rafe's throat. There were too many scents in the room. All familiar. Adri and the five missing fighters.

"Who?" Rafe gasped, his throat closing on the words, his wolf still frantically scenting the air to figure out where their mate was.

"Not him," Silas gritted out, arm muscles bulging as he tackled the shifter in return and fought against the extra strength of his ferality to contain him. Marco sprinted to help him, cursing his second's impulsive move that put him in harm's way.

The snap of the poor kid's neck as Marco joined the fray echoed into an eerie moment of quiet.

"Rafe? You can't be here! Get out!"

Rafe's head snapped toward the voice he would know anywhere, even as slurred and drugged out as Adri sounded. Ignoring his mate's ridiculous instruction, Rafe raced toward his crumpled form chained to the far wall.

"Fuck, kitten. What did they do to you?" Rafe said, dropping to his knees beside his mate and hauling him into his arms. His searching fingers ran across Adri's scalp, and he froze as he felt the telltale dip where his skull had been breached.

Adri's groan of pain had him cursing himself for his carelessness. He'd barely opened his mouth to call for help when Marco was there. He'd found a sledgehammer somewhere, wielding it like it was lighter than air as he smashed the chain's tether from the wall. Scooping his mate and the broken chain up into his arms, Rafe sprinted for the SUV and the makeshift field hospital Emmy had the foresight to set up while everyone else was distracted.

"Adri, where are the rest of them?" Marco asked as Rafe gently placed him on the hastily assembled operating trolley.

"Two of them should be chained nearby. Three turned feral already, pulled their chains from the wall," Adri said, his fist clinging tight to Rafe's jacket.

Rafe pressed a kiss to his jaw and then his lips. "I need to get that chip out of you while we still can, kitten."

His words sparked a new panic in his mate, and Rafe threw himself across Adri's body before he tumbled to the floor.

"They'll detonate it! Get away from me!" Adri cried, voice frantic.

"Kitten. Kitten!" Rafe shouted, forcing Adri to look at him. "I've got you. The *pack's* got you. The signal blocker should last long enough to get you and the other two sorted. They won't be able to do a damn thing."

Adri froze as he processed Rafe's words.

"Do the others first," Adri said.

Rafe's wolf howled in protest inside him. "Sweetheart, I won't be able to focus on a damn thing until you're safe. The sooner I get that chip out of you, the faster I'll be able to help the others."

Adri looked like he might put up a fight, but Marco

leaned in close. "I won't let them die, Carter. Now shut up and let your mate work."

Adri's mouth snapped shut. Then his eyes narrowed in anger as he processed his body's involuntary reaction to their Alpha's order. They didn't have time for any of that, though.

"I'm going to knock you out with my power so you don't have to feel me digging inside your brain, kitten. That okay?" Rafe asked.

Adri's jaguar shone bright in his eyes as he stared up at him. "Of course. I trust you with my life, Rafe. I trust you with everything."

Reaching out before he could overthink it, Rafe let his power flow through him, sending Adri into a deep sleep. To his right, Emmy had already connected the video link to Katie, and the portable floodlights had been set up so she could see what he was doing.

"Take this now. I'll get whatever they've drugged him with out of his system," Luca's mate Cal said, stepping in close from wherever he'd been to press a syringe into Rafe's hand.

Rafe injected the stimulant immediately before sinking into the focus he needed for what was to come. As he extended his awareness into his mate's body, he could feel the water witch's cooling power doing just what he'd said and seeking out the foreign substances in Adri's bloodstream—silver and who knew what else—and drawing them out.

Distantly, he heard the sound of gunfire and yelling, but he couldn't focus on that. Marco would keep them safe.

"Craniotomy?" Rafe asked, hand extended towards Emmy.

The cranial drill was pressed into his palm, and he stared at it blankly for a moment. He'd practised this the other day with Katie. Stood in her kitchen and created perfect circles in a skull stolen from the forgotten in the hospital's morgue.

That skull hadn't been attached to a body more precious to him than life, though. It didn't have soft lips parted slightly in slumber. It didn't have skin he wanted to trace with his fingertips until he had every inch memorised by touch alone.

"Doc? You don't have time for this," Cal said, voice gentle.

Shaking himself, Rafe forced himself into the clinical calm he was so used to, even though it felt like he was dressing up in someone else's ill-fitting suit. He could do this. He *had* to do this.

Turning his mate's beautiful face to the side, he didn't hesitate again as he turned the drill on and reopened the wound he could still feel in the bones there. The world narrowed to the circle of skull he pulled free, to the veins pulsing with his mate's heartbeat as he exposed his brain, to the rivulets of blood as he used a scalpel to excise the technological cancer forced on his mate. And all the time, he channelled his power into his mate—healing the damage to Adri's brain as he sacrificed accuracy for speed; stopping the bleeding from the veins clustered around the chip that would otherwise be trapped in Adri's skull when he closed up the wound; burning away any chance of infection from the unsterile conditions before it could take root… and desperately willing Adri's heart to keep beating when it stuttered under the pressure of two surgeries and whatever poison they'd pumped into his veins to keep him compliant.

"You did it, Doc," Cal finally said, gently pulling the needle from his hand as Rafe stared down at the neat line of stitches on his mate's scalp.

Rafe clung to Adri as someone—Marco—tried to lift him clear.

"Two more to go, Doc," Marco reminded him. "He'll be sad if they don't make it."

Rafe whined in exhaustion and complaint, a noise his wolf forced out through lips still human, before leaning down to press his forehead to Adri's. Two more to go. He'd poured so much of himself into healing Adri, he didn't know if he had anymore to give. Cal silently pushed another of his stimulant syringes into his hand.

"I'll catch you when you fall. Just hang on long enough for them."

Rafe nodded once, turning away from where his Alpha was carrying his soul away from him to focus on his next patient.

CHAPTER 18: ADRI

Adri sat perfectly still on the seat next to the bed, staring down at his mate's face that was too pale, too lax. Rafe never looked so passive, even in sleep. He was dynamic. Dominant. This wasn't right.

Adri had come to twelve hours earlier. Apparently, brain surgery was easier to heal from than magical burnout like Rafe had brought on himself. Adri was wracked with guilt. He'd asked Rafe to heal the others first. It hadn't even occurred to him that his powerful mate would struggle to heal all three. That Adri's request might push Rafe past the limits of his body.

"He's going to be okay."

Adri's head jerked up at Marco's words from the door. He hadn't even heard the Alpha arrive.

"Relax. I'm just dropping you some food."

"Thanks."

They'd been brought back to the Lunetti pack lands, rather than Rafe's apartment, where it was easier to protect them. At least Marco had put them in one of the forest's small cabins instead of the main house, though. Adri didn't think he could have coped with the noise and social expectations of being close to so many nosy wolves.

Stepping closer, Marco gripped his shoulder with a strong hand, passing him a steaming meat pie that had Adri drooling.

"You need to get your strength back. He's not going to be happy if you've stressed yourself into being ill when he wakes."

Not bothering to shrug off Marco's touch, Adri tore into the pie, suddenly aware of his ravenous hunger now that he had food in his hands.

"Good kitten," Marco murmured when he'd finished.

"Hey, only I get to call him that," Rafe said, voice soft and raspy from disuse.

A strangled sob left Adri as he pulled himself away from their Alpha and flew into his mate's arms.

"Oof. Gentle, kitten. It's okay. I've got you."

Adri clung to Rafe as the doc continued his string of reassurances, his trembling hand petting Adri's skin, soothing him with the reassurance that he was finally *there*.

"Don't you ever fucking do that to me again," Adri growled, as he clung even tighter.

"I have no plans to go digging in your brain again if I can help it," Rafe said, pushing himself up until he was sitting.

"Not *that*," Adri snapped, rolling his eyes. "I don't give a shit what you have to do to me to save me. Don't ever *leave me* like that again. Don't go where I can't follow."

"I think I'll leave you two to it. Come find me when you're bonded," Marco murmured, silently sliding out of the cabin and closing the door with a decisive click.

"Come here, kitten," Rafe said, pulling him closer in his arms and entwining their bodies until Adri couldn't tell where he ended and Rafe began. "I'm not going anywhere. I'm *yours*."

Adri nuzzled in under Rafe's jaw, breathing in his scent and grounding himself in his solid calm. His eyes slipped shut as they lay together, revelling in his mate's presence.

"I need everyone to know I'm yours, too."

Rafe's gentle stroking paused. "You mean that, kitten? You're ready to wear my mark for real?"

Adri's words finally caught up with him and his heart rate sped, but it wasn't nerves. It was excitement. He was past ready, but his mate was still burned out.

"You need to eat first. And sleep."

Rafe rolled him onto his back, pinning him to the bed and staring deep into his eyes. "You really mean it?"

Oh, this man. How had Adri made him wait all these years until he couldn't quite believe what was happening? He'd have to make sure Rafe never had any doubts again.

"I've never meant anything more in my life. I want you to fuck me under the moon like you wolves are so keen on, sink those beautiful fangs into my neck, bond us for eternity, and then fill me with your knot until our bodies are as tied together as our souls."

"Even if it means being pack?"

Adri thought of the way Marco had come through for him and his fighters, of the welcome he'd had at the pack run, and the care he'd been shown when he woke scared and confused and howling for his mate the previous day.

"I'm already pack."

"Fuck, I love you," Rafe murmured, pressing a kiss to his lips. "I've loved you for thirteen fucking *years,* and I will love every single breath, every fight, every act of defiance for the rest of our lives."

"What about every act of submission?" Adri asked. "I love you, too." Then he tilted his head and bared his throat to his mate.

Rafe moaned, mouthing at the sensitive skin there. "Fuck,

you're too tempting, kitten. You're going to make me forget I don't have the strength for what I need to do to you."

Adri's brow furrowed in concern, and he rolled Rafe off him so he could go grab another pie from the kitchen. When he turned back, Rafe was watching him with a smile.

"What?"

"My wolf loves that you want to feed us."

Adri huffed a breath and sat back on the bed next to him, breaking off a piece of pastry and meat and pressing it to Rafe's lips instead of handing him the food. Rafe held eye contact as he licked the juices from his fingers before biting down gently. Once he'd finished, Rafe pulled him right back into his arms, like he couldn't bear not having every inch of their skin pressing close from chest to toes. Adri's chest vibrated as he finally let himself relax now that his mate was fed and conscious.

"Are you *purring*, kitten?"

Groaning, Adri hid his face in Rafe's throat, sparking a laugh from the older man. "Can we just go to sleep and pretend my jaguar isn't a total simp for you?"

"Yes, but only because when we wake up, I'm going to devour you."

Adri's purr grew even louder, and Rafe moaned. "That's so hot. Love the noises you make. Love everything about you."

Settling down, Adri let the reassuring noise of Rafe's deepening breaths lull him into sleep. Just before he succumbed, he whispered into his skin, "I love you, too."

Strong arms tightened around him, and Rafe kissed his nape from where he was spooning him. "It means everything that you trust me enough to tell me, kitten. Thank you."

Adri must've been more tired than he thought because when he woke later that night, Rafe was already up and dressed—if you could call low-slung sweatpants and nothing else dressed—as he moved quietly around the cabin, making them coffee. Kicking the covers down, Adri indulged in his jaguar's need to stretch, exaggerating the arch of his back when he felt Rafe's eyes on him.

By silent agreement, they orbited each other at a distance as Adri rolled out of bed and headed to the shower. Poised. Waiting. Like they both knew that the second they touched, it was on. The clink of cutlery was the only noise as they ate breakfast for dinner—fluffy eggs and crusty, thick bread with freshly squeezed orange juice.

Adri had been hard since before he woke, and his cock only ached harder the longer they went without touching. Knowing where this was heading, he'd taken the time to clean and prep in the shower. He hadn't bothered with clothes when he emerged, and Rafe's knowing eyes shone gold with his wolf as he tracked Adri's naked body moving around the space.

"Tell me you want this," Rafe said as Adri stacked their dishes in the sink before turning to lean back and stare at his mate.

Like so often when he didn't brace himself before glancing at Rafe, Adri lost his breath for a moment as he took in his tanned, powerful muscles, the silver-grey of his hair glinting in the light, and his furry chest just begging for Adri to run his fingers over it. It was the look on his face that undid him, though—hope. Affection. Love.

If Rafe needed reassurance every day that Adri was in this, he'd give it. Anything to keep that hopeful, contented look on him. Rafe carried so much past hurt, gave too much of himself to everyone around him. Adri was going to make sure he never had to do it alone again. Rafe had shown him over and over again for more than a decade that he was there for him, and Adri could finally believe that care came with no strings. That Rafe was never going to try to control him in ways he didn't want to be controlled, or stifle the fierce independence of his jaguar.

"Make me yours, Rafe. Bond me so you never doubt how much I need you again. Bond me so I can feel your soul curled up in my chest where it belongs. Bond me so my strength can bolster you when you tire, and my love can carry you through when the pain you see every day is too much."

Rafe opened his mouth like he was going to ask if he was certain again, and then closed it. The tension in the room spiked, and Adri drew in a sharp breath as raw dominance emanated from his mate.

"Then, run," Rafe growled, shoving his sweatpants to the floor and stalking in Adri's direction.

Mouth stretching in a wicked grin, Adri spun lightly on the balls of his feet and tore out of the cabin into the moonlit forest.

CHAPTER 19: RAFE

Rafe's heart sang in his chest as he grabbed the lube and ran after his mate. He'd never seen Adri like this—playful and open. Rafe's mate had been so angry and determined for so long that he'd started wondering if that was just who he was after what happened to him, but deep down, he'd known it could be like this between them. That once Adri processed that he was *safe*, he'd finally be free to pounce and twine and tear through the forest, making trouble. It didn't mean he wouldn't also snap and ambush. It just meant that murderous instinct of his was balanced with something else. Something he'd been missing for too long since he was taken and forced into the fighting ring—love.

If he hadn't already waited thirteen years, maybe Rafe would have dragged this out longer and let Adri lead him a merry chase through the forest. Maybe they would have shifted to their animal forms to stalk each other. There'd be time for that later. Time for that *forever*. Right then, he couldn't bear waiting another second. Desperation rode him hard as he used every bit of his alpha speed to power across the clearing, letting his dominance roll out ahead of him.

In the distance, a wolf howled in raw joy and was answered by others—Marco and the pack. His Alpha could sense what was about to happen through their bond. Rafe ignored it. Ignored everything but the way his mate's scent made his blood run hot, and the tantalising view of his glutes tensing and releasing as he pounded across the grass.

Lunging forward, Rafe wrapped an arm around Adri's waist, spinning to throw him to the ground and twisting at the last second so it was his back that crashed to the ground, and he could cushion Adri's fall. Their bodies slotted together like they were made for each other, and they groaned in unison as their throbbing lengths pressed close. Dropping the lube beside them, Rafe reached up and grabbed Adri's nape, hauling him into a filthy kiss that had his mate breathless and laughing.

"Did you seriously stop to grab lube and still catch me before I got past the edge of the clearing? You didn't need it. I'm ready for you."

Rafe grinned. "I was *highly* motivated. And I'm not going to risk hurting you. Plus, I don't think I can take that ridged monster without a little help."

Adri pulled back, eyes glittering as he stared down at Rafe. "You going to let me take you, Doc?"

"Of course," Rafe said. "Doesn't mean I won't still be in charge, though."

Adri huffed out a breath and leaned down, nipping at his ear with sharp teeth and sparking another moan of pleasure from him. "Only because I *let* you be in charge, and only when we're fucking."

"You're so hot when you let me give you pleasure. And we're not going to be *fucking*."

"What are we doing, then?" Adri asked with a furrowed brow.

"Making love, mating, committing, *breeding*." That last

one made his mate throw his head back on a laugh like he knew it would.

"You gonna put your puppies in my belly, Rafe? Don't think it works like that."

"We'll never know if we don't practise. A lot."

Adri leaned down, pressing a kiss to his lips at the same time as he reached down to stroke his hard length. Rafe's wolf lunged to the forefront of his mind, and raw need flooded his system. Playful was nice, but now he *needed*.

Rolling them in one smooth move, Rafe flipped Adri onto his hands and knees, burying his face between his mate's legs before he could do more than gasp a surprised laugh that quickly turned to desperate panting as Rafe laved over Adri's soft, slippery hole with his tongue. He'd been starving for his mate for thirteen years, and now he was *ravenous*.

Gripping Adri's thick, muscled thighs tight enough to bruise, he ate him out like he'd die if he couldn't devour his mate's taste, like pushing his tongue deep into his mate's body was his sole purpose in life. Reaching around his waist, Rafe started jerking him off frantically at the same time as he used a touch of his power to make sure Adri didn't come. The next time his mate climaxed was going to be on his fucking knot with Rafe's fangs buried in his skin.

"Fuck! Rafe. Please!" Adri moaned, pushing back onto his tongue before thrusting forward into his fist like he couldn't figure out which sensation he'd rather chase. "Need you inside me. Need you to claim me. Don't make me keep begging, Rafe."

Grabbing the lube, Rafe pulled back to slick his fingers, pushing three of them in at once as he monitored his mate's body for any discomfort. His knot would be no joke, but neither of them had the patience for drawn-out foreplay.

"But you're so pretty when you beg, kitten."

Adri snarled at him over his shoulder, and it sent another

shot of lust straight to his dick. Pausing in the moonlit night, Rafe slowed things down, sliding a featherlight hand up his mate's spine until that delicious feline arch grew even deeper, and pressing gently between his shoulders until he dropped his chest right down to the grass.

"Rafe, please," Adri whined, hips shifting as he sought the touch of his mate's body where he needed it most that Rafe was denying him.

No way could he deny his mate's sweet pleading. Pressing the head of his cock to Adri's body, Rafe felt tears gathering in his eyes as he finally, finally, pushed inside. He'd waited so long to feel that tight heat wrapping around him. Waited so long for his mate to choose to submit. A part of him had wondered if Adri would ever be ready. Now, as he pushed inside his body in one perfect, slow thrust, it felt like he was coming home. Overwhelmed by sensation, Rafe could already feel the base of his cock tingling where his knot would form once they bonded.

"Do it," Adri said, pushing back into him.

"Want to make it last," Rafe murmured.

"Next time," Adri said, because there would be a next time, and all the times after.

Reaching down to grab Adri's shoulder, Rafe pulled him more upright. The next time he thrust hard into his mate's body, his lips were brushing close to that perfect, tempting dip where his neck met his shoulder as his balls slapped against his mate's ass.

"Fuck, yes! Right there," Adri whined, his inner muscles gripping Rafe's cock tight as he tried to pull further out again, only to give in and thrust back inside Adri in tight, desperate movements.

With his power, he could feel the way his mate's prostate was being stimulated by every movement of his body. He amped up the sensation until Adri was rutting and desperate beneath him. He might not be able to make this last, but he could make it just as intense and satisfying.

"Love you so much," Rafe said, biting his lip with sharpened fangs as he fought for control.

"So, show me," Adri groaned, tilting his head to the side in a submission as perfect as any wolf would have.

It was too much. He couldn't wait any longer. Leaning in close, Rafe caught Adri's skin between his teeth, biting down almost hard enough to break the skin as he kept up his driving thrusts into his mate's body.

"Please. Bite me. Make me yours. Claim me." Adri's words were becoming more and more slurred as he lost himself to pleasure. It was a thing of beauty to see.

With one final thrust, Rafe finally let his teeth sink into his mate's skin, biting deep and feeling the sweet taste of life-changing, soul-healing blood fill his mouth. His knot swelled impossibly fast as he felt the mate bond click into place between them, and a little piece of Adri take refuge deep inside him where he could hold him close forever. As soon as his teeth pulled clear, Adri was twisting in an impressive demonstration of feline flexibility, and his jaguar's teeth sank into the skin over his pec, right above his heart. Pleasure like he'd never known flooded his body as their orgasms rocked through them, his vision whiting out as he sank into ecstasy.

When they finally came back to themselves, they were a tangled mess of limbs and sweat on the grass. Rafe nuzzled in close to Adri's neck, mouthing over the quickly healing mate bite that would show his mark as a silver scar forever.

"I'm impressed you managed to bite that deep into my chest," he murmured with a smile.

Adri twisted to press a kiss to his lips, tugging at them with his teeth. "Yeah, well. I'm not a wolf and I'm not going to bite like one."

"You're perfect."

"You don't mind?" Adri asked softly.

Rafe almost wished his knot would deflate faster so he could turn his mate over and see him better for this, but the thought was fleeting as the throbbing pleasure of Adri's body gripping his length distracted him. They were wrapped so tightly around each other that they didn't need to be face-to-face. Plus, Rafe could feel his mate's reassuring presence deep inside now. Could feel the cautious, fragile hope Adri had for this thing between them.

"I love it. I love you. Can you feel how much?" Rafe asked, pushing every emotion he was feeling down the bond toward his mate until Adri's eyes turned wide and his mouth trembled.

"You … I had no idea," Adri said.

Rafe grumbled against his mate's skin, thrusting his hips a little to feel his body convulse around him. "I know. I waited so long for you to realise. Now you never need to doubt again."

"Are you pouting?" Adri asked with a smile.

Rafe's knot finally started to deflate, and he pulled out of his mate's body with a groan, flipping Adri onto his back before caging him in with his arms on either side of his head. "I don't pout."

Adri grinned. "Does my big, bad, alpha wolf need to feel how much I want you again?"

And that was enough of that.

"Nice try, kitten," Rafe said, raising himself up on his knees and grabbing the lube so he could slick his fingers.

"What are you doing, Doc?" Adri asked, cocking his head.

Rafe groaned as he pushed two fingers inside himself, using a touch of his power to ease the stretch faster before notching Adri's cock against his body and sinking back down onto it.

"Fuck!" Adri shouted, bucking up into him as the delicious burn of his hole stretching around each and every one of those delightful ridges rocked him with desire.

Pushing one hand to Adri's shoulder, and another to his hip, Rafe pinned his mate to the ground and started riding him in earnest, refusing to let Adri do anything but take it, take *him*. Adri's hands clenched into fists by his sides like he knew Rafe wasn't going to let him get away with touching.

Fuck, Adri was so good for him.

"That's it, kitten. Just like that. You feel fucking amazing."

"Rafe, please."

"Please, what?" Did his mate want to take charge? Rafe would give him anything he wanted.

"Please make me come."

Rafe's eyes rolled back in pleasure as he squeezed tight around Adri's cock, milking him as he rode him. "Come for me, kitten," he cried, his power flowing through them both to rip their climaxes from them.

The sensation of his mate's cum filling his body was everything, and his hand drifted down Adri's chest, pinching at his nipple as he rode him to completion. Rafe's cock jerked in the air, untouched, red and throbbing as he shot ropes of cum all over his mate's body, marking him. It wasn't enough. Nothing would ever be enough.

As soon as Adri's shivers of pleasure started to subside, Rafe raised himself up, wincing in complaint as he felt the absence of his mate from his body before slinging one of Adri's legs over his shoulder and shoving back inside him.

This time, he let Adri move with him as he fucked him into the ground, revelling in the way his mate's eyes had rolled back in his head as his body tensed with pleasure. The bond between them was sharing every sensation between them in a never-ending crescendo of raw desire and ecstasy.

"Holy fuck. How many times are you going to make us

come?" Adri moaned, already riding the edge of another climax as Rafe pounded into him.

Sweat dripped from his body to Adri's despite the chill air as Rafe's mouth twitched in a filthy smirk.

"*All* the times. And in between, I'm going to take you home and make sure you never want for anything ever again."

"You already do that for me. You always have. You promised me once that you would always be here for me. That you would always come when I call. Now, I'm going to do the same for you. Forever," Adri said, wrapping his legs around Rafe's waist and lifting his head to draw him into a deep kiss as their lovemaking turned slower and deeper.

It was everything Rafe had always wanted. Everything Adri had defied for so many years. It was just *everything*.

CHAPTER 20: MARCO

The familiar bittersweet ache of watching his pack find their mates hit hard as Marco sat at his desk, taking in the couples filling the room. Sassy vampire Vin, who his grumpy head of security, Angelo, had fallen so hard for despite himself. Cal, who'd healed the broken pieces of Luca's heart that Marco had never quite managed to touch. The searing heat burning between Emmy and his biker witch Rocco. And their newest pairing. The one he'd been rooting for the longest. Their doc had finally seduced his cagey jaguar, and it was everything it had promised to be.

"Forever looks good on you, Doc," Marco said, eyes trailing down to the telltale bulge in Adri's pants as he sat on his mate's lap.

"Alpha," Rafe said, warning in his tone, and Marco tipped his head in silent apology.

It wasn't that he would ever try to insert himself into their relationships; it's just that he could feel some of what they were feeling through the pack bonds he had with each of them. It was enough to drive his wolf crazy. There was a hole deep inside him that he kept hidden where his own mate had lived—and died—before they could bond. He would defend these pairs with his dying breath to protect what they had together, and he would crave it to his dying breath just as much.

"Did we learn anything from the other fighters?" Marco asked, turning to Silas, who'd stepped in to support the rescued guys while Adri was distracted with his mating, as he should be.

Adri straightened where he sat, leaning forward with predatory focus and a heavy side of guilt.

"They were held longer than Adri, so they saw more. They reported multiple staging areas in the tunnel system and the scents of way more shifters than we knew about."

"Are they building a fucking feral *army*?" Marco growled. Everyone in the room looked horrified at the possibility.

"Some kind of army, anyway. The mayor said something while they were holding me—that we'd either be feral or under their control. I think the chips do more than we've seen so far," Adri said.

"So, the mayor is definitely involved? He's dropped off our radar." Marco hadn't wanted to interrupt their bonding time to question Carter earlier. He'd trusted his newest packmate would've alerted them to anything urgent.

"I've got Seth keeping an eye out for him," Emmy chimed in.

Marco's focus narrowed on his cousin, Alpha instinct sending a chill across his skin. "Who?"

"One of my informants—a vampire."

Marco trusted his family. Did his best not to micromanage them, but something about the energy coming from his cousin was setting off a silent alarm.

"Tell me," he ordered.

"How about I show you?" Emmy said with a smirk.

Pushing to his feet, Marco stalked over to his cousin, grabbing his phone from his hand and scrolling through a handful of photos there. Rage filled him as he took them in—the emaciated body, the bruises, the shadow of fear in his eyes. He was too fragile for this world.

"Who the fuck did this to him?" Marco growled, low and dangerous.

"He was turned a few years ago for Kyan's sex trade. Works for one of the pimps on the west side."

"Is he even legal? And why hasn't he healed?"

"He's twenty-five. They're keeping him hungry to slow his recovery," Rafe said. He didn't bother explaining why they'd do that, but they all knew. There were some sick fucks out there in the city.

Marco swapped his focus to the doc. "Were you there when these were taken? Did you heal him?"

"I couldn't. They'd kill him if they found out his association with the pack."

"So, offer him fucking sanctuary, then!"

"We tried, but he wasn't having it. He doesn't trust supernaturals. For good reason. I'm sure some of his Johns are shifters, and they probably have no love for vampires. He thinks if he can just survive long enough, he'll earn a safer place with his own kind," Emmy said.

"Fuck that. I'm bringing him home," Marco snapped, striding straight out the door.

Everything else could wait. The tortured pain in those haunting, silver doe eyes could not.

Thanks for reading! The final book in the series is Marco and Seth's HIS MATE BY DOMINANCE.

ABOUT THE AUTHOR

Mel Aitchess writes MM paranormal romance with a bite. She loves delicious enemies to lovers tension, possessive men who burn for each other without being alphaholes, and supernatural suspense that keeps you turning the page.

You can find her and sign up for her newsletter at: www.melaitchess.com or join Mel's Patreon, Mel Aitchess MM Bite Club, at https://patreon.com/MelAitchess.

www.ingramcontent.com/pod-product-compliance
Lightning Source LLC
LaVergne TN
LVHW091052080826
845145LV00002B/722